THE CRY

Nicola Page is keen to get the job as Staff Nurse at
the Meadowlands Rehabilitation Centre until she
finds that Simon Grey—who belongs firmly in her
past—is on the board of interviewers. If she accepts
the job will she once more be running headlong into
heartache?

THE CRY OF THE SWAN

BY
SARAH FRANKLIN

MILLS & BOON LIMITED
London · Sydney · Toronto

First published in Great Britain 1984
by Mills & Boon Limited, 15–16 Brook's Mews,
London W1A 1DR

© Sarah Franklin 1984

Australian copyright 1984
Philippine copyright 1984

ISBN 0 263 74571 6

Set in 11 on 12½ pt Linotron Times
03/0284–52,164

Photoset by Rowland Phototypesetting Ltd
Bury St Edmunds, Suffolk
Made and printed in Great Britain by
Richard Clay (The Chaucer Press) Ltd
Bungay, Suffolk

CHAPTER ONE

NICOLA looked at her watch. The last candidate had been called in for her interview ages ago—or so it seemed. They must be taking them in alphabetical order, she supposed, but at least there could not be much longer to wait.

It was a pleasant room, large but well proportioned. A refreshing breeze wafted in through the long window that looked out onto a lawn and there was a bowl of roses on the polished round table in the centre of the room. There was also a pile of magazines, but Nicola had leafed unseeing through them all. She looked again at her watch. Surely that last interview must be over by now. Could they have forgotten about her? At this rate Laura would be home before she was. She half rose to walk over to the window, but at the same moment the door opened and the pretty young secretary appeared. Nicola looked hopefully at her.

'I'm sorry you've been kept waiting,' the girl said. 'But if you'd like to come this way—' she held the door for Nicola to pass through in front of her. They crossed the hall and she saw that the interview was to be conducted in Sister's office, the door of which was ajar. The girl looked at the notepad in her hand.

'Let's see, it's Miss Page, isn't it?'

Nicola nodded, her mouth dry. She hated interviews. Somehow she never seemed to be at her best at them.

The girl went in ahead and announced her. Nicola took a deep breath and walked into the room, hoping that she looked more confident than she felt.

Sister's desk had been pushed back to make more room and round it sat three people. One of them, Sister Martin, whom Nicola remembered slightly from her training days at Bishop's Wood Hospital, was now 'Matron' here at Meadowlands Rehabilitation Centre. She smiled reassuringly at Nicola and motioned to her to be seated, but Nicola didn't have to be told twice to sit down. She had just received a shock. Sinking onto the chair provided she tried hard not to stare at the tall man seated in the centre of the three.

She was stunned. It was four years since she had set eyes on Simon Grey. When she left Bishop's Wood she had thought she would never see him again. Would he remember her, she wondered? There was really no reason why he should. In those days he had been a senior registrar—tipped for an early consultancy—she, a mere student nurse. Simon's work was with plastic surgery, and in Casualty and later, working as staff nurse on Intensive Care she had had the early care of many of his patients. She had seen then how brilliant he was, how dedicated and caring.

Suddenly she looked up with a start, aware that he was speaking to her.

'I see here that your main experience has been in Intensive Care. What prompted you to apply for a job where the work will obviously be so different?'

He looked older—perhaps even more than four years older. The dark hair, though as thick and smooth as ever, was now frosted with silver. His grey eyes were more serious and thoughtful and there were new lines about his mouth. Nicola cleared her throat in an effort to relax the tightened muscles.

'I wanted a change—something where I could have more personal contact with the patients,' she told him. 'In Intensive Care they come to us immediately after admission, as you know, and stay for only two or three days. Often they are unconscious or heavily sedated, which means that they don't even remember us afterwards.'

Simon smiled at her and her heart gave a painful lurch. His smile was exactly as she remembered it. 'And you like to be remembered, do you?' he asked.

She blushed. 'It isn't so much that—just that it's rewarding, seeing one's patients getting well and going home.'

Simon looked down at his notes. 'You know, of course, that Meadowlands is a rehabilitation centre for patients disabled in accidents who have no families to support them through the difficult period of readjustment.' He looked up at her. 'Will you tell us something about your own family background, Miss Page?'

She moistened her dry lips. 'I have one brother, a

little older than me. Our parents both died when we were quite young and we were brought up by a distant cousin who is now a health visitor. She lives quite near here, at Milton Green.'

Sister Martin smiled. 'So you feel that you would have a special understanding of people who are left alone in the world?'

Nicola nodded. 'Very much so—although of course I have been lucky.'

The third member of the interviewing board asked Nicola some questions about her education and training, explaining that he was from the administration side. All the time she was answering she felt Simon's eyes on her until eventually he said:

'I'm still not clear, Miss Page, why it is that you have chosen this particular kind of work. Intensive Care demands a very strict routine while in this work you will find yourself required to rely on instinct a great deal. You're not the emotional type, I hope?'

Nicola shook her head, her colour mounting.

'Good. And I hope you don't visualise it as a romantic kind of job. Because I can assure you that it isn't.'

She resented the remark. Surely he knew that she had been in nursing long enough to realise that there were very few branches of it that could be termed 'romantic'.

'Certainly not, Mr Grey,' she said firmly. 'I have enjoyed my period in Intensive Care and I think I have learned a lot from it. But I feel I have more to offer—as a person as well as a nurse—than carrying out a strict routine, however vital.'

He looked up at her and his eyes held hers for a long moment—until she could bear their steady gaze no longer and looked away.

'I see. Well, I'm sure that's very commendable of you.' Was there a hint of sarcasm in his tone? He looked again at the notes before him. 'And of course the New Forest is perhaps a pleasanter place than the city of Leeds—and conveniently close to your cousin too?' He looked up at her enquiringly, one eyebrow slightly raised.

'That's true, though it had nothing to do with my reason for applying,' Nicola told him truthfully. 'My cousin drew my attention to the advertisement after she had heard me saying I wanted a change.'

Finally it was Simon himself who rose from his seat to see her to the door. She had forgotten how tall he was—towering above her as he opened it for her.

'Thank you very much for coming, Miss Page,' he said with studied politeness. 'You will, of course, be hearing from us again in due course.'

As she looked up at him he smiled again and all the way back to Milton Green the smile stayed tantalisingly behind her eyelids, as though imprinted there, so that every time she closed her eyes she could see it again.

The bus ambled its way along the leafy roads at a leisurely pace, leaving Nicola plenty of time for thought. When Laura had suggested that she apply for the job at Meadowlands had she known that

Simon Grey would be on the board of interviewers, or was the whole thing just a remarkable coincidence? Had she remembered that he and Nicola had been at Bishop's Wood at the same time?

The late afternoon sunshine made the bus warm and airless and Nicola closed her eyes, allowing her thoughts to drift. Seeing Simon again like that had been a shock—in more ways than one. Four years was a long time and she had thought it all behind her. She supposed an onlooker at the time would have called what she felt for Simon a young girl's crush on an older, married man but she knew now, just as she had then, that it was much, *much* more. She had been quite hopelessly in love. All the past four years had done was to blur the sharp edges, numb the pain, but this afternoon at the interview it had been rekindled like a match held to dry tinder.

She wondered again about Laura. On her frequent visits to the cottage at weekends she had complained to her cousin of her longing for a change and it had been Laura who had sent the cutting from the local paper along with the advertisement from the nursing journal for a staff nurse for the new rehabilitation centre. Nicola remembered the letter she had enclosed with it: 'I happen to know that they're looking for someone young,' Laura had written. 'And you said you were looking for a complete change. This is just the thing for you. Get cracking—apply for it!' It was so typical of Laura. She always thought she knew exactly what was best. But Nicola had to admit that in the past she had often proved right.

She had decided to apply. Chris, the young pharmacist she had been going out with for the past few months, had begun to talk claustrophobically of engagement rings and mortgages. Yes—it was time for a change. She liked the sound of the job very much and the place, Meadowlands, a converted house set in several acres of rolling New Forest parkland, was delightful. After working in the noise and heat of the city it would have seemed like heaven to her—except that now she knew she couldn't possibly take the job even if it were offered to her. It could only lead to inevitable heartbreak.

Closing her eyes again she had a vision of Simon's lovely wife Claudia with her shining black hair and vibrant Italian beauty. There was the little girl too—Maria. Nicola had nursed her once, when she was still a student and the child had been admitted with appendicitis. She must be quite a young lady by now. Everyone had always remarked what an ideal family they were, so wrapped up in one another, so devoted. Nicola had looked on enviously, wondering what it would be like to be loved by a man like Simon—to be the one woman in the whole world he cared for above all others. A hopeless dream, but none the less real and painful for all that. It was what she had been running from when she had escaped to Leeds. She could not allow herself to go through that all over again.

The bus, which had moved onto the by-pass for the last three miles of the journey, was turning off now to rumble over the little bridge into the market place at Milton Green. Nicola got up and waited for it to come to a halt outside Johnson's the bakers. As she stepped down the scent of freshly baked bread and doughnuts—Johnson's speciality—assailed her nostrils, reminding her sharply of her childhood. On impulse she slipped into the shop to buy some for tea. It would help to soften the blow when she told Laura that she would not, after all, be taking the job at Meadowlands.

A cacophany of barking greeted her as she opened the creaky front gate and the moment she let herself into the cottage Laura's two dogs hurled themselves ecstatically at her. Sheena, the labrador, placed two huge paws on her shoulders and proceeded to lick her face while Herbert, the dachshund, had to content himself with running in circles round her feet and pawing at her tights. She put down her handbag and the bag of doughnuts and set about the business of calming them. They were dreadfully spoilt. Laura had never made the slightest attempt at training them in the proper social behaviour and it was certainly too late to do anything about it now. She had just persuaded them to run out into the back garden when she heard the familiar chugging of Laura's Mini and a moment later Laura herself rushed in in much the same effusive manner as the dogs.

'Ah—so you beat me to it! Well—how did it go? Do you like the place? They say it's really marvellous—wonderful views and everything. When would you have to start? Would you be living in or could you come home?' Laura's spectacles gleamed with enthusiasm as she pulled off her coat and began to roll up her sleeves and unpack the bulging bag of shopping she had brought in with her. Nicola laughed.

'Shall I take your questions in alphabetical order or will chronological do?'

Laura tossed a packet of butter into the fridge and turned to her with a sigh. 'Oh—sorry, love. It's just that I've been thinking about you all afternoon—*willing* you to get the job. It'd be so lovely to have you nearer home again. Is that terribly selfish of me?'

'Of course it isn't. It's nice to think someone cares about me,' Nicola smiled. 'But I really haven't a clue whether or not I've got the job and, to be honest, Laura, I don't think I could take it.'

The smile vanished from Laura's face and she sat down heavily at the kitchen table. 'Oh—that is bad news. Why though? Didn't the place appeal to you? I'd have thought it'd be just what you'd like.'

Nicola sat down opposite her. 'It is—it's just—' She glanced up at Laura. 'Did you know that Simon Grey would be there this afternoon?'

Laura looked surprised. 'Well, yes, of course. He would be, wouldn't he? I mean, Meadowlands used to be his home. I thought you knew that.'

It was Nicola's turn to be surprised. 'His home?'

Laura nodded. 'His family home, anyway. He inherited it when his father died, but it seems he didn't fancy living there so he donated it to the NHS with the proviso that it be turned into a rehabilitation centre for homeless RTA victims.'

'I see. He gave the whole estate?'

'Not all. I believe he lives in a small dower house in the grounds. He's a consultant at Medchester General now, of course, but he keeps an eye on Meadowlands too. I dare say many of the patients there will be his own.'

Nicola looked at her cousin closely. 'You *did* remember that he was at Bishop's Wood at the same time as me, didn't you?'

Laura blinked vaguely. 'Yes, that's right, I suppose he would be. But what does that have to do with—oh—' She peered at Nicola anxiously. 'Was he the one you had that terrible crush on? But that was all so long ago—surely you don't still—' She sighed. 'Oh dear. I've put my foot in it, haven't I?'

Nicola shook her head unhappily. 'I know it sounds ridiculous but when I walked into that room this afternoon and saw him again I knew it wasn't over at all. I'm afraid that going there to work—coming into constant contact with him again—would be asking for trouble.'

Laura frowned. 'Surely it wouldn't be as tragic as you seem to think.'

Nicola sighed patiently. 'You surely must remember that Simon is married,' she said. 'He has a beautiful Italian wife—I believe she's a talented artist. And they have a small daughter, Maria. Don't you remember her? She had appendicitis when I was on the children's ward at Bishop's Wood.'

'Well of course I know all that,' Laura snapped impatiently. 'But surely you heard?'

'Heard—heard what?' Nicola shook her head. Laura really could be maddening at times.

'That he lost his wife two years ago,' Laura said. 'Claudia Grey was killed in a tragic car crash. It was a terrible night and her car went off the road on that bad bend just outside Farthingbridge. She must have been driving much too fast. That was why he gave up the house—and I dare say it was his reason for devoting it to accident victims. They do say—'

But Nicola wasn't listening. Instead she kept remembering Simon's face, the way the merriment had gone from his eyes and the new lines around his mouth—lines of suffering? Everyone had always said how much in love he had been with his beautiful wife, Claudia. What a terrible thing to have happened to him.

'And his daughter?' she heard herself asking. 'What happened to Maria?'

Laura stopped in mid-sentence. 'I believe she lives with him at the Dower House. I seem to have heard somewhere that the woman who used to be the child's nanny stayed on as housekeeper. They—' She rose to her feet, staring out of the window. 'What's that the dogs are squabbling over on the lawn?'

Nicola joined her at the window and gave a cry of dismay. 'Oh *no*! It's the bag of doughnuts!'

Much later that night, as Nicola lay in bed she thought again of Simon's tragedy and what it must have meant to him. It was strange, she reflected, the cards that life dealt sometimes. Four years ago Simon had everything—a brilliant career ahead of him, a beautiful and talented wife, a delightful small daughter and the prospect of a stately family home. Then suddenly a stretch of greasy road, a small error of judgment, and it was all gone—wiped out in an instant. How must he have felt? Would he ever fully recover? What a good thing he still had Maria. He would have to make the best of life, if only for her sake. Behind her closed eyelids she could still see his face, handsome but aloof, as though only part of him were there. Deep inside she longed to be able to help him—somehow to ease his pain. If she were lucky enough to be offered the job at Meadowlands might she perhaps find an opportunity to do that?

She turned over impatiently, thumping her pillow. How presumptuous of her to think that *she* could be of any help to him. Why, he didn't even remember her! Her mind drifted back to her student days at Bishop's Wood. The very first time she had set eyes on Simon Grey she had fallen in love with him. The way his dark grey eyes twinkled when he smiled and the lift at the corners of the wide, sensitive mouth. He had such a sense of fun in those days, and yet there was such compassion in his strong hands when he tended the patients. That first Christmas they had put on a concert for staff and patients. She had played with Simon in one of the sketches. It was the only time there had ever been physical contact between them and she could remember it still—his eyes laughing down into hers and his arm, so warm and firm around her waist.

Angrily she threw back the covers and got out of

bed to walk to the window. She really must pull
herself together. She was fantasising like a four-
teen-year-old! Her life and Simon's had always
been poles apart, always had been and, as far as she
could see, always would. It was utterly ridiculous
for her to be thinking in this way. The best thing she
could do would be to get back to Leeds as soon as
possible—forget all about Meadowlands—even
marry Chris if he asked her, she told herself desperately.

It was ten days later that she got the letter. She
read it twice to make sure she wasn't imagining it.
She was offered the job of staff nurse at Meadowlands. It would be appreciated if she could start at
the beginning of next month and living-in accom-
modation would be provided. Suddenly Nicola was
faced with the reality of making the decision.

All that day she worked automatically—check-
ing monitors—taking two-hourly blood samples.
She prepared for a new admission to the ward, a
post operative RTA case with severe head and
chest injuries and later, as she watched the patient,
a young woman, struggle for life, hanging on by a
thread, she thought of Claudia Grey. Had Simon
had the trauma of seeing his wife like this—breathing with the aid of a ventilator, heavily sedated,
bruised and disfigured? By the end of the day as she
went off duty she had made her decision. She would
give in her notice and take the job at Meadowlands.
If there was a way—any way at all—that she could
make Simon smile again she would do it. Maybe
she was a fool; maybe she was running headlong

into heartbreak again, but if she didn't take this chance she would never know—and that was something she couldn't live with.

CHAPTER TWO

NICOLA put away the last of her clothes in the roomy wardrobe and looked around her. The flat at Meadowlands was spacious and airy, consisting of a sitting room, bedroom with adjoining bathroom and a tiny kitchenette where she could prepare her own meals whenever she wanted. She had never had such a completely self-contained place of her own before and she looked forward to enjoying the luxury of it.

It had been a long day. She had left Leeds by an early train—seen off by a bewildered Chris who still couldn't understand why she wanted to change her job.

'I understand what you mean about not being ready for marriage,' he told her earnestly. 'But I don't see why you have to go away. I wouldn't have bothered you. We could still have been friends.'

She looked at him with a small ache in her heart. He was so sweet and she knew all too well what it was like to be in love with someone who couldn't return that love.

'Chris—it's better this way,' she told him gently. 'I really appreciate your friendship but I don't deserve it. I can't give back all that you're prepared to give me and it isn't fair. It wouldn't work for either of us.' But the memory of his anguished face

19

haunted her throughout the long journey. For the past four years it had been the same with each new relationship she had embarked on. Better not to make any more new male friends, she told herself firmly.

With a sigh she walked over to the window to look out at the view. The flat was on the first floor and had an uninterrupted vista of rolling New Forest heath. The colours were breathtaking: golden yellow gorse, purple heather and the rich tender green of new bracken fronds. The air was heavy with the scent of pine and peat and she breathed it in appreciatively. Below her lay a small garden at the rear of the house. Smooth green lawns were bordered with a shrubbery planted thickly with rhododendron, azalea and hydrangeas in every shade of blue and pink. She decided it would make the perfect place to relax when she was off duty.

When she had first arrived she had been met by Sister Martin. The middle-aged Sister remembered Nicola from her early days at Bishop's Wood where she had been a Sister Tutor. Together they had made a tour of Meadowlands and Nicola had been introduced to the other members of the staff.

'We can accommodate eight patients at present,' Sister told her, 'although there are plans for extending the place, then we shall be able to take a dozen or more. As you know, most serious cases are discharged from hospital as soon as possible, coming back daily for treatment and therapy, the idea being that the family environment is best for their readjustment and recovery.'

'But when they have no family or relative willing to help there is a serious problem,' Nicola added. 'Places like Meadowlands are vital to cases like that.'

Sister Martin nodded as she led the way up the main staircase. 'That's right. It will be a great relief to have you living in here. I live in Farthingbridge and of course I have my husband to care for. This is really a sort of semi-retirement job for me. Until now I've had to spend most of my nights here. You see, apart from ourselves the rest of the staff are auxiliaries—not counting the physio and the occupational therapist who come in each day, of course.' She smiled at Nicola. 'I'm very glad to have someone I know to work with, but I thought you were going to specialise in Intensive Care.'

'I did for a while,' Nicola told her. 'And I enjoyed it very much, but I have felt for some time that I needed a change, one that would bring me into more personal contact with the patients.

Sister Martin smiled ruefully. 'You'll certainly achieve that here. It will be a very big change from Intensive Care. I hope you don't find it too much of a contrast. The work can be very demanding—and, at times quite harrowing.' She opened the door of a room that was furnished as a lounge. 'This is the TV room,' she explained. 'Of course there is a lift for the patients who can't manage the stairs. It's quiet at the moment because at this time of day the patients are usually resting in their rooms. It might be a good time for you to meet them individually. Come along.'

Nicola followed her along a corridor. Sister stopped in front of a door. 'This one is Gerry Armstrong,' she said quietly. 'He was a budding motorcycle champion until both legs were badly crushed in a bad track accident. He has been in a wheelchair but he's just beginning to walk again with help and, mark my words, we're going to have problems with him!'

Nicola looked puzzled. 'Forgive me for asking, but wouldn't it have been better for him to have had a room on the ground floor?'

Sister shook her head. 'When he first came to us he was very depressed and bitter. If his room had been too accessible he would have stayed in it all day long. He had months of micro-surgery and careful nursing to save his legs and it's a miracle that he's able to walk at all, but you try telling him that! He had his heart set on making that championship and if he can't—' She lifted her shoulders. 'Well—I need hardly say more, need I?'

Gerry sat at a table by the window doing a jig-saw puzzle and when Sister Martin introduced Nicola he grinned cheekily.

'Well—things are definitely looking up. It'll be nice to have a bit of glamour around the place, eh, Sister?' he said with a twinkle.

Sister Martin pursed her lips. 'Don't let Staff Nurse Page's looks fool you,' she warned. 'She did her training under me and, believe me, she can be as stern as I can, so don't try any of your tricks on her!'

As she closed the door Sister smiled at Nicola.

'He's quite a handful. We're trying to convince him that he should learn a new trade. Maybe you'll have more success than I have with him.' She shook her head. 'Maybe now you can see what you're taking on.'

Nicola was introduced to Frank, who had lost an arm in an accident that had taken his wife and son from him; Jim, a young lorry driver, paralysed after a motorway pile-up and Mary, the middle-aged victim of a hit-and-run driver. But for her the most harrowing was Natalie, who, at twenty-three had had her hopes of a modelling career dashed when her face had been badly burned. Sister explained that Simon Grey had done extensive skin grafts but that the girl's confidence had been shattered.

'Perhaps you can see what Meadowlands means to these people,' Sister told her later as they talked over tea in her office. 'When they come to us they're broken in spirit as well as in body. As well as learning a new trade or skill they must learn to cope with the day-to-day business of caring for themselves if they're not to become institutionalised.' Sister stood up smiling. 'Now, I'd like to introduce you to two of the nicest people you're ever likely to meet: Ted and Marjorie Shelford, our cook and handyman. They live here too, in the flat above yours at the back of the house. They have a special sympathy with what we're trying to do here. Two years ago Mr Grey saved the life of their only son when he was involved in a bad accident on the building site where he worked. He's fine now, but they've never forgotten how much he needed them when he was recovering.' She smiled. 'But I've no doubt they'll tell you all about that themselves. I'm sure you'll like them both.'

Nicola found that she was right. Marjorie was a plump, motherly woman who welcomed her smilingly into a spotless kitchen where she and her husband, Ted were sitting down to their afternoon tea.

'I hope you'll feel free to come and talk to me anytime, dear,' she said in her rich West Country lilt. 'I'm not one of those who likes the kitchen to myself. The more the merrier, I always say. If there's anything you want any help with or if you're lonely and fancy a chat, well, you know where I am. You'll usually find me here.'

Ted, a small, wiry man with bright, brown eyes looked up with a smile. 'She likes a chat all right—not to mention a good gossip!'

'What a thing to say, Ted Shelford!' His wife looked scandalised. 'You'll be giving Staff Nurse Page here all the wrong ideas about me!' She smiled apologetically at Nicola. 'Maybe Sister has told you—Ted and I live here, so when you have days or evenings off you've no need to worry. We have a "hot line" to Mr Grey's house too, just in case of emergencies.'

It was the first time Nicola had heard his name mentioned since her arrival and her heart skipped a beat. She wondered how often he visited Meadowlands but she couldn't bring herself to ask. Marjorie hurried on:

'Now—what are you doing about your supper,

dear? I know you won't have had time to get anything in. Why don't you come down here and have yours with Ted and me? It won't be anything fancy, just cold ham and salad, but you're more than welcome.'

Nicola smiled. 'Thank you, Mrs Shelford. That would be very nice.' Something about the woman's personality made her feel at home—almost as though she were already settled in.

Upstairs in her flat she took out her uniform and hung it up, ready for the morning, then she changed into jeans and a t-shirt and ran a comb through her short fair hair. For a long moment she stood regarding her reflection in the mirror, making a critical assessment of herself. Slim build, medium height—she sighed. She must be about the most average girl possible! Eyes a sort of nondescript green, hair, honey blonde, though it did curl naturally. What chance had she of attracting a man like Simon Grey? she asked herself despairingly. She remembered vividly Claudia Grey's dark, dramatic looks, her raven black hair and wand-slim figure. Any woman would have difficulty living up to her image. With a sigh she began to arrange her personal belongings about the room. If she was to make it her home she wanted it to reflect her personality as much as possible.

'Do you come from a big family, dear?' Marjorie heaped her plate with new potatoes fragrant with mint until Nicola held up her hand, laughing.

'Please—that's plenty. No, there's only my brother and myself. We were brought up by a distant cousin after our parents were killed in a plane crash when we were both quite small.'

Marjorie's face creased with concern. 'Oh—you poor little dears. I'm sorry.'

'It was a very long time ago and we were both too young to realise what had happened at the time,' Nicola told her. 'Laura had never married and I like to think that Terry and I made up to her a little for that. We were the family she never had.'

'I see, so she's a lot older than you?' Marjorie passed the salad bowl.

'Yes, she's a health visitor and she lives at Milton Green. I hope to see a lot more of her now that I'm so near.'

'How nice. I'm sure she'll be pleased about that.' Marjorie pushed a dish of mayonnaise across the table. 'Do have some dressing, dear. It's home-made.' She watched with satisfaction as Nicola helped herself. 'It's nice that you'll be working with Sister Martin again, isn't it?' she observed. 'You won't feel so strange, having someone here who you know.'

'Mr Grey was at Bishop's Wood Hospital at the same time as me too.' Nicola felt her cheeks colouring as she said it. She was well aware that she was encouraging Marjorie to gossip and she felt slightly ashamed of the fact.

'Well, well! So you've worked with him before too? Ah, he's a lovely man and such a clever doctor, though I think you may find him rather changed since you knew him.' She shook her head.

'I'll always swear that our boy wouldn't be alive today if it hadn't been for him.' She looked across at her husband. 'Isn't that what we always say, Ted?' Ted nodded, his mouth full and Marjorie went on: 'Four years ago, I think you said that was. You would have known his poor wife then?'

Nicola looked at her plate. 'Yes—she was very beautiful.'

Marjorie shook her head. 'So I've heard tell. A terrible tragedy, that was. It was just after that that our Billy had his accident, but Mr Grey didn't allow his grief to stop him helping others. Poor dear man. I dare say his work helped him. You know, ever since it happened he seems to work non-stop. A lonely life it must be, living there with that poor child.'

'Poor child?' Nicola queried, looking up. 'Is she—'

'Didn't you know—she was in the car with her mother at the time of the accident,' Marjorie told her in a hushed whisper. 'A bit of a mystery it was really, with it being so late at night and everything. At first they thought she might have suffered some brain damage—nasty head injury she had. Never uttered a word for weeks—but no. All the tests were negative, thank God. It was the shock that had left her withdrawn. Couldn't remember a thing. What is it they call it—am—am—?'

'Amnesia,' Ted supplied, pushing his empty plate away.

'That's it. They say she still can't remember a thing about the accident, but that's just as well, poor little love, though the rest of her memory came back all right.' She shook her head. 'Ah yes, that poor man has had more than his share of trouble. That was why Ted and I jumped at the chance to come here and work for him. It was all we could think of to help pay him back for what he did for us.'

Ted laid down his knife and fork and looked across to Nicola. 'Nurse Page must be wondering how it is we know so much about Mr Grey and his affairs,' he said. 'She'll be thinking we're a right pair of old busybodies!'

'Caring about people isn't being a busybody!' Marjorie said defensively. 'But as it happens my best friend is Mr Grey's housekeeper, Maud Dickens, and she keeps me in touch, so to speak.'

Nicola's head was spinning. Poor Simon. He certainly had had his share of trouble. Had it really changed him, she wondered. Could he ever be the same person again. Aloud she said:

'Some people do seem to get more than they deserve, don't they?' She pushed her empty plate away. 'Thank you for supper. It was delicious.'

'I'm so glad you enjoyed it. Ted grows all the vegetables here you know. A dab hand he is at gardening.'

Ted got to his feet. 'That reminds me. I've got some watering to do in the greenhouse this evening. You'll have to take Betsy for her walk.' He pushed his chair back from the table and went to the door. As he opened it a tiny Yorkshire terrier ran in to fuss round Marjorie's feet. She picked up the little dog and looked at her husband reproachfully.

'*I* can't take her. You brought me in that great basket of vegetables to blanch for the freezer. It'll take me all evening.'

'Please—let me take her,' Nicola begged. 'I'm used to dogs. My cousin has two. If you just give me her collar and lead—'

Marjorie looked at her gratefully. 'Oh, that would be a help, dear. She does so look forward to her walk.'

'I shall enjoy it,' Nicola assured her. 'And it'll give me the chance to explore a little. I haven't seen much yet except the inside of the house.'

Betsy was a friendly little dog and clearly not fussy about who took her for her evening walk. She trotted happily along in front of Nicola at the end of her lead. A slight haze was rising from the ground after the day's heat and as Nicola let herself through the gate in the garden wall the view that met her eyes made her stand and stare. Beyond the grounds of Meadowlands lay the vast expanse of heath she had seen from her window and now the evening breeze brought the scent of it to her nostrils. In the distance the trees gathered thickly, blurred a misty blue by the fading evening light whilst the sky shone with a pearly irridescence that reminded her that the sea was only a handful of miles away. Something about the atmosphere and the tang in the air lightened her spirits as she stepped out across the spongy turf, stooping now to let Betsy off her lead so that she could enjoy the freedom too.

She never knew where the big grey dog came from. He seemed to materialise out of the shadows like a shaggy grey ghost, loping up to Betsy, catching her easily and rolling her over and over with his huge nose. The little dog gave a series of frightened squeaks as Nicola watched, appalled. What would she say to Marjorie if this great brute hurt her? She leapt forward to scoop up the tiny dog, but she wasn't quite quick enough. Betsy took off as fast as her little legs would carry her, the large shaggy dog in hot pursuit and Nicola following and calling:

'Betsy! Come back here!' She stopped short as she rounded a clump of trees in time to see Betsy disappearing under a tall yew hedge while the big dog ran up and down, looking for a gap large enough to allow him to follow. Her heart in her mouth, Nicola ran along the hedge looking for a gate. She found one and let herself in, looking round feverishly and calling Betsy's name whilst she searched the dense shrubbery. She heard twigs snapping and bent to look under a laurel bush, hoping to find Betsy cowering there, but at the same moment a hand grasped the collar of her shirt and hauled her out roughly.

'What do you think you're doing? Don't you know you're on private property?' The voice was angry and Nicola gasped as she was hauled unceremoniously to her feet and twisted round.

'Good God—it's you!' Simon Grey was as startled as she to find himself looking into her frightened eyes. He let her go at once. 'I'm sorry—I thought it was one of the village lads after my fruit again. I hope I didn't hurt you.'

'No—it's all right—I mean, it's I who should apologise,' Nicola stammered breathlessly. 'I was taking Mrs Shelford's dog for a walk when a huge grey dog chased her. I was afraid he might do her some damage, so when she ran under your hedge—'

Simon laughed. 'Oh, that would be Seamus. You needn't have worried, he and Betsy are old friends, but he plays rather roughly with her sometimes.' He pointed. 'Look, there she is—she's quite all right.'

With relief Nicola saw that Betsy was at her feet. She picked her up and looked at Simon. 'I'm sorry for trespassing. I'll be getting back now.' As though from nowhere the big grey dog appeared again and Simon took hold of his collar.

'Time you came in for the night, old fellow,' he said. He looked at Nicola. 'You still look shaken. Will you come in and let me give you a drink?'

She shook her head. 'Oh no—I don't want to intrude—'

'You won't. In fact you'll save me a journey. I was coming to see you anyway.' He didn't wait for her to answer but led the way out of the shrubbery.

Now that she had time to look around her she saw that she was in the garden of a small house. Old fashioned plants grew in profusion under apple and plum trees: lavender, stocks, tobacco plant and honeysuckle; their scents mingling exotically on the evening air. They crossed a small lawn with a gnarled mulberry tree in its centre and Nicola saw the house. A roof of weathered plum-coloured tiles swept low over whitewashed walls, giving the leaded windows a sleepy-eyed look. Simon led the way in through the open french windows and Nicola found herself in a long, low-ceilinged room. It looked comfortable and lived-in. He indicated an armchair, still holding the dog's collar.

'Please—have a seat. I'll put Seamus in the kitchen and then you can relax.'

She sat on the edge of one of the armchairs and looked around her. On the mantelpiece was a photograph of a little girl taken with the big grey dog. It was Maria, she recognised the large brown eyes and dark hair though she looked older and more grown up since Nicola had last seen her. Simon came back into the room and went to the sideboard.

'I can offer you a sherry—or would you prefer brandy?'

'No—sherry will be fine, thank you.' She was wondering if there was any particular reason why he had intended to come and see her. He crossed the room and handed her a glass, then stood with his back to the fireplace, looking down at her, his face unsmiling.

'This is quite a good opportunity for me to have a private word with you,' he said. 'There is something I'd like to have clear between us from the start.' He took a sip from the brandy glass he held, then his eyes swept coldly over her face. 'I think it only right that you should know that I was against your being appointed. I'll be honest with you—the job was offered to another candidate first, but she turned it down.'

There was a silence that seemed to last an eternity. Nicola felt oddly detached, noticing small things like the ticking of the clock and the pattern on the carpet. She looked up at Simon, her heart contracting as she noticed the fine veins on the back of the hand that held the glass, the tension in the knuckles, a muscle twitching at the corner of his mouth—then, slowly she registered what he had just said. She was only really here by chance—and against his better judgment. Her fingers tightened round the stem of her glass and she cleared her throat.

'I see. May I know why, please?'

He turned away, his face stony. 'There are several reasons—one is that I simply didn't consider you experienced enough. Intensive Care is very different from the kind of work and the problems you'll encounter here.'

'But that is the very reason I applied,' she put in eagerly. 'I'm looking forward to the change—and to gaining new experience.'

He turned to look at her again and she saw that his eyes held what appeared to her like something approaching scorn.

'This isn't a training establishment. That is just the point I'm trying to make. We simply can't afford to take nurses on a hit and miss basis.'

Stung, she rose and put her unfinished drink on the mantelpiece. 'I'm sorry you feel that way, Mr

Grey,' she said, her throat tight with hurt. 'As we worked together at Bishop's Wood I thought—' she swallowed, 'I *flattered* myself that you considered me a good enough nurse to take up the challenge here at Meadowlands. But perhaps you didn't even remember me anyway. I'm sorry I was forced upon you against your wishes but I shall just have to do my best to keep out of your way. Goodnight.' She walked out of the room through the french windows with as much dignity as she could manage, but as she was halfway across the lawn a voice stopped her:

'Wait—you're forgetting something!'

She stopped and turned to see him coming towards her with Betsy in his arms. 'You're forgetting Marjorie's dog—here.' He placed the little dog in her outstretched arms.

'Oh—thank you.' She turned away again without raising her eyes to his but he placed a hand on her shoulder.

'I didn't mean to offend you—or to cast any aspersions on your nursing skills,' he said quietly.

'Didn't you?' Nicola said sharply. 'Then I wonder what your reason was for speaking as you did!' She looked up at him and for a moment her eyes held his.

'I believe in being honest,' he said coolly. 'I'm afraid I rather distrust people who want to change horses in mid-stream, especially where the welfare of others is at stake.'

The hurt she felt inside suddenly erupted into anger. It was totally arrogant of him to assume that he knew her motives for taking this job. She drew a deep breath and looked straight into his eyes.

'I don't happen to believe that the welfare of anyone is at stake, Mr Grey,' she told him coldly. 'And I hardly think that in trying to expand my experience I am being fickle. The only thing I can suggest is that if you find my work inadequate in any way you should take steps to have me dismissed.'

He gave an audible gasp and opened his mouth as though to snap back at her, then closed it again. 'As I have already said, your nursing ability is not in question,' he said with controlled patience. 'There are—other reasons for my objection to your appointment—reasons that do not concern you personally and that I can't go into. I was merely trying to be straight with you about my position in the matter.'

She looked up at him steadily. 'What you are really saying is that if I have to be here you would prefer it if you didn't have to see too much of me.'

An expression of irritation crossed his face. 'No, I'm certainly *not* saying that! You seem hell bent on misunderstanding everything I say!'

Without another word she turned and walked away from him across the lawn, through the shrubbery and out through the gate without once looking back. On the walk back to Meadowlands her mind seethed with resentment. What right had he to speak to her like that? And what *were* the 'other objections' he had mentioned? If they did not concern her personally it was unfair to hold her responsible for them. Marjorie had certainly been right when she had said he was a changed man! And to think that she—Nicola—had come here full of noble intentions! '*If I can make him smile again!*' she muttered derisively to herself. 'I must have been *mad*!'

CHAPTER THREE

NICOLA slept badly. Once her anger had worn off depression set in. She despised herself and the idealistic picture she had built up of herself helping Simon Grey to rebuild his life. What a fool she had been—like some silly schoolgirl with a crush on a pop star. But as drowsiness overtook her another part of her consciousness was seeing Simon as he stood before his own fireplace earlier that evening; his eyes, distant and cool, the strength and magic in his hands, the line of his jaw and the new relentlessness of his mouth. Her memory lingered around that mouth, something deep inside her longing for the power to soften those hard lips with a kiss. With an aching despair she knew that no matter what he said or did she would never stop feeling like this.

With a sudden impatient movement she was awake again. He was not for her—now or ever! And the sooner she got that fact into her head, the better. In fact the best thing she could do would be to keep well out of his way. The very sight of her seemed to upset him for some reason or other. But of one thing she was certain: she would show him that he had been wrong about her. She would do the best job she could here at Meadowlands and make him eat his words if it was the last thing she ever did!

She slipped easily into the routine at Meadowlands and in the first few days there was plenty to do, getting to know the patients and the other members of staff; the care assistants who came in daily on a shift basis, the occupational therapist, Mary Graham, and Geoff Carter, the physio. She got along well with the patients, especially Gerry Armstrong, who seemed to have taken it upon himself to make her feel at home, finding excuses to attract her attention whenever he could. Now that he was on his feet again it was a continual job keeping track of him and stopping him from overdoing things. She had been at Meadowlands about ten days when she caught him out of his wheelchair and setting off down the drive towards the main gate one morning. Shaking her head she set off after him.

'Hey—Gerry! Where do you think you're going?'

He turned towards her with a sigh. 'Can't a guy do *anything* without a woman running after him?' He gave a sigh of mock despair. 'If only I wasn't so damned irresistible!'

Nicola took his arm firmly, shaking her head and trying not to smile. 'You had a really strenuous physio session this morning and you know perfectly well that you should be resting now before lunch. No sense in rushing things. Anyway—where *were* you going?'

He gave her his impish grin. 'I thought I'd have a look at the village. I've heard all about it but I've never seen it yet. There's bound to be a pub—might come in useful to know where the nearest civilisation is!'

Nicola looked at him regretfully. 'Sorry, Gerry. You know we can't let you do that yet. Be patient a little longer. Tell you what—on my next day off I'll take you.'

His eyes lit up for a moment, then clouded again. 'Oh—you mean in the tumbril. You have to be joking! Think I'd let myself be seen being pushed like some old crock in that thing—and by a girl?'

'I'm afraid it's that or nothing,' she told him. 'Maybe we could leave the chair somewhere and you could walk the last small stretch into the village. Will that do?'

He grinned wryly. 'Have to, I suppose. You're not a bad sort really, Staff—thanks.' He peered at her. 'But what about the pub? You wouldn't stop me from having a drink, would you?'

She laughed. 'Well, I don't suppose a small one would be objected to, though we'll have to check, of course. As it was my free time I might even join you. How's that?'

He raised an eyebrow. 'Wow! Better watch it, Staff—can't have you being nicked by the local fuzz for being drunk in charge of a tumbril!'

She smiled. 'I can assure you there's no danger of that. Now, let's get you up to your room. You've still time for a short nap before lunch.' She knew he would insist on trying to walk up the stairs instead of taking the lift, but he deliberately pretended to misunderstand:

'You're always in such a hurry to get me up to my

room, Staff,' he said with a twinkle. 'I shall begin to think you fancy me soon! I think it's wicked to take advantage of a man in my state of health!'

Nicola bit her lip hard in an effort not to laugh. 'If you don't behave I shall have to ask Sister to take you,' she admonished.

He stuck out his lower lip. 'That's what I *call* taking advantage—blackmail, that is!'

They were still conducting this good-natured form of banter as they passed the door of Sister's office. Suddenly it opened and she came out, accompanied by Simon Grey. It was the first time she had seen him since that first evening when they had crossed swords and Nicola felt her heart quicken. Gerry looked up with a grin.

'Hi, Doc. I was on my way out to the pub but I got recaptured. I'm thinking of starting a tunnel next week. Want to be on the escape committee?'

Simon gave him a rueful smile. 'Hard luck. Take it easy though, Gerry. You know, unlike some, you'll eventually make it out of here on your own two feet. You don't want to do anything to spoil your chances of that, do you?'

'No chance with bloodhounds like Staff here about the place,' Gerry told him. 'But she isn't a bad sort really. She's even promised to take me boozing on her next day off.'

Simon transferred his gaze to Nicola, one eyebrow slightly raised. She felt her colour change as he said: 'Really? How kind of her.'

'I haven't lost the old charm, you see, Doc,' Gerry went on as Nicola's face turned scarlet. 'I can still pull the birds. I think the limp brings out the mother in them!'

Nicola almost pushed him towards the lift. 'Come *on*—time we got you upstairs,' she said between clenched teeth.

'See what I mean, Doc?' Gerry called cheerfully over his shoulder. 'She can't wait to get me alone!'

Nicola frowned crossly at him as the lift door closed. 'Do you have to be so brash, Gerry? Fancy talking to Mr Grey like that! I told you I'd have to *check* whether I could take you out first!'

He pulled a face at her. 'Well—thought I might cheer him up. Looks as if he could do with a good laugh. He's got a face as long as a fisherman's wellie most of the time!'

'He has good reason with patients like you about the place disrupting everything,' she told him. 'Now, let's have no more out of you until lunch, or that trip I promised you is definitely off!'

As soon as he was settled Nicola ran down the stairs and out into the garden. Simon was chatting to Frank who had been helping Ted Shelford in the greenhouses and she caught him just as he was turning away.

'Mr Grey—could I have a word, please?' she called.

He turned his head and stood waiting for her to catch up, glancing at his watch with ill-disguised impatience.

'I won't keep you,' she assured him. 'I just wanted to check with you that it's all right if I take Gerry Armstrong into the village on my next day off. You see I thought it might be a good opportunity to talk to him on a less formal plane—about his future, I mean. Away from the—'

'You really don't have to justify your actions to me,' he interrupted. 'Gerry Armstrong isn't my patient and what you choose to do in your free time is none of my business.'

She stared at him. 'You don't understand. I've been trying to get Gerry to face the fact that he'll never race again—to think about taking up an alternative career.'

'Very commendable, I'm sure. Now, if you'll excuse me, I have a patient to see.'

She stood her ground, determined this time not to be crushed by his churlish attitude. 'Forgive me if I have the wrong idea, but I thought that the whole idea of Meadowlands was that we were supposed to take the place of the patients' family—to help in a personal, as well as a medical way.'

'Up to a point. We do still have the services of the hospital social workers to call upon,' he pointed out. 'It is a mistake to allow yourself to become personally involved. That's where professionalism comes in, as I'm sure your training will have taught you.'

'I see—then you feel it would be wrong for me to take Gerry out into the village?'

He sighed. 'I didn't say that. Just be careful. Compassion is one thing; it's practical and constructive. Sympathy is something else. It can make for complications.' He looked at his watch again. 'And now I really must go.'

She watched helplessly as he strode across the lawn to where his car was parked on the driveway, then, with a shrug, she made her way back towards the house. Sister Martin was in the hall as she came in.

'Ah, there you are, Staff. Mr Grey was here to see Natalie. He's worried about her progress. She's still so depressed, poor child. He tells me he's going to try some laser treatment for her scars, to assist the healing. I'm sure it would make a world of difference if she could see some improvement taking place.

'That's good,' Nicola said abstractedly.

Sister looked at her closely, 'Is anything the matter?'

Nicola bit her lip. 'It's just that I don't seem to be able to do anything right for Mr Grey. I was afraid after what Gerry said that he would think I was taking him on some sort of riotous binge so I went after him to explain. But he seemed to misunderstand quite deliberately.'

Sister shook her head. 'He's still a very unhappy man, my dear. He has bad days sometimes. You must make allowances.'

'But there's no need to take it out on me!' Nicola said vehemently. 'I know he was against my appointment here too.'

Sister looked at her sharply. 'Who told you that?'

'He did! He seems to think that wanting a change is a sign of instability.'

Sister frowned. 'I thought he was quite pleased with the appointment. It's true that you weren't the first choice. It was offered to another candidate because she had had quite extensive experience in this field. But when she declined and you were suggested as second choice Mr Grey made no objection that I knew of.'

'Nevertheless, he has made it clear that he disapproves of me,' Nicola said, her throat tight. 'It doesn't make my work here any easier.'

Sister opened her mouth to say something else but just at that moment the lunch bell sounded and they both hurried in the direction of the dining room.

Nicola's day off was the following Thursday and at breakfast time Gerry reminded her of her promise to him.

'Hey, Staff—it's today, isn't it?' He winked saucily at her, then leaned across the table to Jim. 'Staff and I are going to paint Farthingbridge red this morning—well perhaps more of a shocking pink—but at least I'm getting out to a real pub for a while. Great, eh?'

Jim looked up with a wistful smile. 'Yes, great. Some people have all the luck.'

Nicola touched his shoulder. 'There's no favouritism about it, Jim. You know I'll take you too if you like, next week.' She looked round the table. 'And that goes for all of you.'

'No thanks,' Jim said proudly. 'I don't think I'm quite ready for it yet.'

She knew what he meant without his having to explain. A burly, athletic young man who had always had the strength of an ox, he was taking time to adjust to being paraplegic. Nicola gave his shoulder a friendly pat.

'Well, when you do feel ready, just let me know. I've been hearing things about Farthingbridge. It seems to have quite a lot going for it. There's a good darts team at the Feathers by all accounts; there's amateur dramatics and a choir that has quite a reputation in the West Country, then there's—'

'Come off it, Staff,' Jim said. 'You'll have me joining the Women's Institute next—learning to knit!'

'And what would be so terrible about that, may I ask?' Mary put in. 'At least you'd be doing something useful instead of sitting there feeling sorry for yourself all day long!' She snorted exasperatedly. 'Men! You're all the same. Pig-headed pride, that's all it is. There are lots of feminine things I'll never do again but I don't sit here brooding about them.'

'Now, now! That'll be quite enough bickering for today,' Nicola said breezily. 'Sister will be on her own today and you don't want to give her any trouble, I'm sure.'

Mary and Jim looked slightly shame-faced and she smiled at them. Privately she agreed with Mary. She had shown a lot of courage since her accident, especially as in the circumstances it looked as though she wouldn't get any compensation. Jim, on the other hand, had refused even the help of Mary Graham, the occupational therapist.

As she went out of the room she caught sight of Natalie reading the morning paper in a corner by the window where she liked to sit, away from all the others.

'Natalie, why don't you come down to the village with Gerry and me?' she invited.

Natalie shook her head. 'Thanks, but I'd rather not.'

'It's market day today,' Nicola told her. 'I'm told it's a very good market.'

'It's a pity it isn't a hundred years ago. I could have got a job in a travelling freak show,' Natalie retorted bitterly. She lifted her head to look at Nicola and her long dark hair fell back from her face. Nicola's heart twisted with pity. The left side, from forehead to chin, had been affected by the burn and although the skin grafts had taken well that side of her face still had a taut, stretched appearance, pink and shiny. It would improve considerably, of course, but nothing would convince Natalie of this. For the rest of her life she would carry facial scars and to her it didn't matter how slight they were. Her life was ruined and nothing would persuade her otherwise. Looking down at her now, Nicola reflected sadly that the thing that marred her face most was nothing to do with her injuries. It was the expression of unhappy dissatisfaction in the large brown eyes. If only she could get her to see this.

'Please come,' she begged, ignoring the bitter remark. 'I've heard there are some interesting people at the market on Thursdays. A young couple from Milton Green run a pottery and they have a stall there. Wouldn't you like to come and see for yourself? Then we could all have a drink and a sandwich at the Feathers afterwards.'

But Natalie didn't reply. Instead she got up, pushing rudely past the others to get to the door. Nicola started to go after her but Gerry shook his head at her.

'Leave her, Staff,' he said softly. 'I've tried to laugh her out of it but it isn't any good. I know what she's going through, poor kid, but she's the sort who has to cope with it in her own way.'

Nicola nodded. This was a new side of Gerry and she approved. He wasn't all brashness after all.

After a walk round the village and a visit to the market they went into the bar of the Feathers for the highlight of Gerry's morning. It was quiet, the rush would be on later when the market folk began to come in for lunch. Gerry insisted on going up to the bar himself for the drinks and refused to accept Nicola's request for a lemonade.

'You're having a pint, like me,' he told her. 'I didn't mean what I said about being drunk in charge—anyway, I don't go out with birds who drink lemonade!'

She laughed. 'All right then, make it a shandy— but half, not a pint.'

He grinned with satisfaction as he put the drinks on the table and sat down opposite her. 'This is the life, eh? At this rate I'll be back on the track in no time!'

She took a sip of her drink and looked at him over the rim of her glass. There was an air of jaunty confidence about him and yet she had begun to realise that much of the time he was whistling in the dark.

'Gerry, I was going to talk to you about that,' she began. 'I think you should start seriously considering a new career. You're young and—'

He put down his glass with a bump. 'Let's get one thing clear, Staff. There is no other career for me. Racing is all I ever wanted. I'm not clever—I was a bit of a dud at school. There was a time when I thought I'd never amount to anything, then, when I was sixteen I rode my first bike and I knew.' He shook his head at her. 'It's hard to describe to you, but out there on the track with a good machine under me it's a whole world of magic. Knowing I've got it together—that I can be better than all the rest. It makes everything worthwhile.'

Nicola sighed. 'One more injury to those legs, Gerry and you might never walk again.'

He grinned and took a pull at his drink. 'I know that. The doc' that fixed me up told me in no uncertain terms. But if I could just make the championship it'd be worth it—to me anyway.'

She shook her head angrily. 'Don't be such a fool. I used to work in Intensive Care. If you'd seen some of the accident cases I've nursed—'

'Okay, okay, spare me the gory details!'

For a few seconds they looked at each other in silence, then he said: 'I suppose Doc Grey's been telling you to work the feminine wiles on me. Right, what do you suggest, a nice office desk, nine till five every day?'

'There are other kinds of jobs, Gerry,' she ventured. 'Mr Grey was right yesterday when he said that you are luckier than the others. You'll have to be careful of your legs, of course, but you won't be disabled like Mary and Jim or even Frank.'

He raised an eyebrow. 'Is that what you were telling Natalie this morning? If so I'm not surprised she won't have anything to do with you!'

Suddenly she saw that he had a point. There were other ways of being disabled besides being paralysed or losing a limb. She bit her lip. Maybe she had been approaching things in the wrong way. She had a lot to learn, it seemed. Could Simon have been right when he doubted her suitability for this job. Gerry reached across to squeeze her hand.

'Don't take it to heart, Staff. It was a nice try and I do appreciate the trouble you lot go to for me. I suppose this is all in the line of duty for you—the softening-up process, but if I can't race I'd just as soon be dead.'

She sighed. 'I don't suppose it's any use telling you that hours and hours of skill and care went into making your legs whole again,' she said resignedly.

He grinned his infectious grin. 'I'm grateful for that. But I just don't feel I have to repay it by living to be a ninety-year-old has-been.' He drained his glass. 'And I don't suppose it's any use asking you if I'm allowed a refill?'

She laughed. 'Not the slightest!'

'Right then.' He got to his feet. 'Tell you what I'll do—I'll give *you* a ride back to Meadowlands in the tumbril. How'd that be for a change?' The old brashness was back and Nicola knew instinctively that all hope of serious conversation was at an end for the day. But she had learned that there were hidden depths to Gerry and the knowledge gave her hope for his future.

On the way back he behaved badly, insisting on walking much further than was good for him. He reminded Nicola of a headstrong toddler and in the end she decided that she must treat him as such.

'Get back into this wheelchair at once, Gerry,' she demanded as firmly as she could. 'Quite apart from anything else the time is getting on and this is my day off, remember!'

'Ah!' He eyed her mischievously. 'Got a date, have we? Who is he then? Some tall, dark, handsome doctor, I'll be bound!'

'As a matter of fact my "date" happens to be short and plump with glasses and *she* is also my cousin, if you must know!'

'Don't believe a word of it! Super looking bird like you—there has to be a feller somewhere,' he teased maddeningly.

'Even if there were it wouldn't be any business of yours,' she told him sternly. 'Now—are you going to get back into the chair or not?'

He laughed. 'Got you on the raw now, haven't I? Look, come on, be a sport—get in and let me give you a push. Go on, just for fun, there's no one to see.' He took her arm but she shrugged him off crossly.

'Gerry! For heaven's sake be your age. I certainly shan't bring you out again if you're going to behave like this!'

But he laughed all the louder and grasped her playfully round the waist, trying to force her back into the wheelchair. Suddenly she heard a car coming round the bend and before she could do anything about it it had swept past them, sending up a cloud of dust from the dry country road. Quite without warning Gerry stopped misbehaving and sat submissively in his chair, his face contrite.

'Sorry, Staff.'

She looked at him. 'What is it—are you in pain?'

He shook his head. 'No—I'm fine.'

She began to push him. 'I don't believe you. Your legs hurt, don't they? I knew you'd overdo it. Maybe that will teach you that you're not ready for that kind of fooling around,' she told him. 'What ever the driver of that car must have thought I don't—' She stopped in mid-sentence as they rounded the bend and saw that the car that had passed them had pulled up at the side of the road. The driver was getting out and she heard Gerry swear softly under his breath.

Simon Grey turned to face them, his mouth set in a grim line. 'I think I'd better give both of you a lift back to Meadowlands, don't you?' he asked.

'It's quite all right—' Nicola began, while Gerry said at the same time:

'It was all my fault, Doc. I thought I'd—'

'I don't think I want to hear,' Simon interrupted. 'I take it you've been on that jaunt you were telling me about.'

'I only had one,' Gerry protested. 'Staff here

wouldn't let me have any more.' But Simon was helping him firmly out of the wheelchair and into the back of the car. Silently Nicola folded the chair and got into the passenger seat. There didn't seem any point in saying anything so she remained silent. Simon drove back to the house without another word, his face expressionless. When they arrived he helped Gerry inside, then looked at her.

'It's your day off, isn't it?'

'Yes—I was going over to Milton Green for the afternoon.'

'I see. Get back into the car then. I'll drop you off at the bus stop. I'm going that way.'

'It's quite all right. I can walk.'

He looked at her stonily. 'I realise that. I'm asking because I want to talk to you. Please get in.'

Her heart sank. Another lecture? As she settled herself back in the passenger seat she wondered how anyone could have changed so. Four years ago Simon had been almost as full of fun as Gerry— now he was more like a character from a Victorian melodrama! She turned to steal a look at him and her heart gave a jerk as she saw that he was having difficulty keeping his face straight. He glanced at her, the corners of his mouth twitching.

'Giving you a hard time, was he?'

She nodded, blushing, almost weak with relief. 'It's rather like trying to cope with a twelve-stone infant!'

He laughed out loud. 'That was why I behaved as I did. He needs discipline and lots of it. But you can't help admiring him after what he's been through.'

'The trouble is I don't think anyone will be able to stop him from having to go through it all over again,' she said despairingly.

He shrugged. 'All we can do is try. When it comes down to it what right have we to tell him what to do with his life anyway?'

She turned to him indignantly. 'But all the work—the care that's been lavished on him.'

He shook his head. 'It's our job. We can't do less—the rest is up to him.'

Just for a moment she caught a glimpse of the old Simon. The fire of enthusiasm and ambition that used to burn in the grey eyes still smouldered there, but now there was something else—a new, deeper understanding—a resigned acceptance. Suddenly she felt close to him, proud to be able to share this one small thing. She swallowed hard, looking down at her hands.

'I suppose so,' she said inadequately.

The car drew to a smooth halt at the bus stop and he turned to look at her. 'Are you staying the night at Milton Green?'

She shook her head. 'No, just having tea with my cousin, Laura Frencham.'

'Of course. I'd forgotten that you were related,' he said. 'Nicola—will you let me give you dinner this evening?'

She gulped, looking into his eyes with a startled expression. He smiled ruefully.

'Oh dear! I asked for that look, didn't I? Look, I

haven't been very nice to you since your arrival here. This is my way of trying to put it right. Will you come?'

He had a shatteringly frank way of putting things. 'There's no need for that,' she said stiffly. 'I'm not a child. I can take criticism along with the best. I'm glad you told me where I stood in your opinion.'

He winced. 'Oh—it's worse than I thought. I *did* upset you.' He looked at her with eyes that melted every resolve, every excuse that came to mind. 'Please—I *want* to take you out to dinner, Nicola. We started off on the wrong foot and it was my fault. Let me put it right, eh?'

She wasn't sure whether he was sending her up slightly, so she said quickly: 'Thank you. I'd like to go.'

'Fine, that's settled then. I'll pick you up at Laura's at, seven?'

She nodded. 'I'll be ready.'

She got out of the car and watched him drive away with a dazed feeling. Nicola! He had called her Nicola! And he was taking her out to dinner— tonight. Just when she had decided that he had become a totally different man from the one she had fallen in love with four years ago he had proved her wrong. Under that new stern exterior the magic charm was still there, perhaps more potent than ever. She glanced at her watch. It was one o'clock. There were six whole hours to wait. They were going to feel more like six years!

CHAPTER FOUR

'TRY A piece of this cake, Nicky. I got the recipe from Mrs Thompson next door. It's bound to be bursting with rotten calories, but never mind.' Laura peered at Nicola. 'That's the fourth time in the past hour!' she said suddenly.

They were sitting in the garden and Nicola looked up with a start. 'Fourth time I've done what?'

'Looked at your watch. It isn't very flattering, you know. Well—do you want a piece of cake or not?'

Nicola smiled apologetically. 'I'm sorry, Laura. Yes please, though only a small piece. I'm going out to dinner later.'

Laura's eyes lit up with interest. 'Dinner eh? Anyone I know?'

'Well yes, as a matter of fact it's Simon Grey. I was just wondering if there was anything suitable I could wear in the wardrobe upstairs.'

Laura put down her cup smartly and raised her eyebrows. 'I thought you and he were at logger-heads. Last time you spoke to me on the phone you said he was finding fault with everything you did!'

'He was—but we met by accident this afternoon and he apologised—asked if he could take me out to dinner by way of making it up to me.'

'And you said yes?' Laura pulled a face. 'Honestly, Nicky, you shouldn't let him get away with it so easily. Some of these doctors think they're God's gift!'

'Simon isn't like that, Laura. Sister Martin says he's still very unhappy about his wife's death. And I'm sure he overworks to take his mind off his problems. Not all the patients at Meadowlands are his and yet he takes a personal interest in everyone.'

'And you're as batty about him as you were when you were twenty,' Laura put in bluntly.

Nicola directed her attention to the cake on her plate. 'Not *batty*. I should hope I've grown up a little since those days. But if I could do something to help—if I could make him as light-hearted as he used to be in the old days—'

'Rubbish!'

Nicola looked up in surprise at Laura's explosive remark. 'What?'

'Rubbish!' Laura repeated. 'It's like I said— you're still batty about him. You *want* him and sooner you're honest with yourself about it, the better! All these altruistic notions you've persuaded yourself into believing aren't healthy. The last person you should try to fool is yourself!'

Nicola stood up, brushing the cake crumbs from her skirt. 'You don't pull any punches, Laura, you never did, but you can't be right every time, you know.'

'Who says I can't?' Laura stuck out her chin aggressively as she gathered up the tea things. 'I've always believed in being straight with people—part of my job. Anyway, you and I are too close for pussyfooting.' She straightened and looked Nicola in the eye. 'I'm right, aren't I? Go on—admit it.'

'I—don't know,' Nicola hedged. 'I suppose I've never really known Simon—*really* known him, I mean. He was just a sort of fantasy figure—unattainable. Anyway, he's changed now. We both have. It's a whole new scene.'

Laura picked up the tray and marched into the house. 'Yes—maybe it's a good job you're getting this chance of getting him out of your system,' she said, 'But don't be disappointed if you find that your idol has feet of clay. There aren't too many fairytale princes about these days!'

Upstairs in her old room Nicola searched the wardrobe, Laura's brutally harsh words echoing uncomfortably in her mind. Deep down she knew that what she was saying was common sense, yet she pushed away the cold realities. Just for tonight she wanted to cling on to her illusions—to believe that Simon was everything she'd always dreamed him to be. After all, it may only be this once. Surely everyone was entitled to one dream-come-true in a lifetime, even if it was partly make-believe.

Right at the back of the wardrobe she found the dress. She had bought it for her brother Terry's engagement party and never worn it because Terry's girl had called the engagement off at the last minute. She pulled it out and held it against herself. It was made of a soft floating material in a deep garnet red that accentuated her fair skin and hair. Quite plain, with a tight-fitting bodice and scooped neckline, it flared softly over the hips. With a little thrill of excitement she dug into the wardrobe again to find the black strappy sandals she had bought to go with it. Little had she known when she had put them away unworn that she would be getting them out to wear on her first date with Simon!

An hour later, at a few minutes to seven, she emerged, ready for the evening. Laura looked up from her knitting and her eyebrows almost disappeared into her hair.

'Well! I hope he appreciates the trouble you've gone to on his behalf! You look good enough for the pages of a fashion magazine!'

Nicola laughed. 'The dress is last year's. It's the one I bought for Terry's engagement party, remember?'

Laura sighed. 'Do I not! I don't know where I went wrong with you two but you have the most complicated and inhibited love lives of anyone I know! Not to mention Terry taking a degree in psychology and then ending up making musical instruments.'

There was no time for Nicola to argue Terry's case. At that moment the doorbell rang. Simon was right on time. Nicola's heart leapt into her throat and she threw a panic-stricken look at Laura who put down her knitting with a sigh.

'All right, I'll go. And for heaven's sake, child, take your heart off your sleeve. It's making you lop-sided!' As she passed she patted Nicola's cheek, her sharp eyes softening. 'Enjoy yourself, honey, but please don't let yourself get hurt,' she said softly.

Simon looked handsome and elegant in a dark grey suit and as he smiled at her his eyes showed clearly that the trouble she had gone to in dressing for him had not been in vain. They drove in silence for the first few minutes and Nicola searched her mind feverishly for some intelligent remark. When at last she thought of something to say she found herself speaking at the same time as Simon. She blushed and shook her head.

'Sorry—what were you about to say?'

'No, you first.'

'It was nothing really—just—I was noticing how beautiful the sunset was this evening. There are no sunsets quite as lovely as the Forest ones. I suppose it has something to do with the reflection from the sea and—and—' she trailed off, feeling stupid and self-conscious. She knew almost nothing about this man, she reflected desperately. Laura had been right: she had built up a sort of fairytale image of him all these years, but she had no idea what he was really like. Maybe he never even noticed things like sunsets—maybe they would turn out to have nothing whatever in common. She glanced at him. He had made some reply to her remark but she hadn't even heard it. Now he was looking at her expectantly as though he expected a response.

'Sorry—?'

'I was just saying that I was glad you liked the sea and sunsets because I've booked a table at the

Harbour Club. I used to go sailing there and I'm still a member, though I haven't sailed since—for some time. It should be very pleasant there this evening.'

'Oh, I'm sure it will, but you really shouldn't have gone to so much trouble.'

'It's the least I can do,' he told her. 'Clearly I was quite wrong about you. Sister tells me that you have a natural flair with the patients and that they've taken to you. Well, I could see that for myself,' he smiled. 'Perhaps I've grown too used to making snap judgments in my work and I'm afraid I'm a little out of practice when it comes to personalities.'

She glanced at his profile, slightly at a loss for words. What exactly did he mean? But at least he was honest enough to admit that he had been wrong. Dared she probe further? She decided to wait until later.

The Harbour Club was on a rocky stretch of road a few miles east of Poole and from the large windows of the restaurant there was a breathtaking view of the bay. The sun was going down in a blaze of glory, sinking into the sea out of a sky streaked with crimson and pearl. Nicola could hardly take her eyes from the sight. Simon ordered the seafood cocktail for which he told her the club was famous and as she ate it she wondered whether this had been a place that Claudia had enjoyed. Almost without thinking she said:

'I only heard recently about your—loss. I'm sorry.'

He glanced up with a look of surprise. 'Thank you. It's over two years now.'

'These things take time though,' she said. 'I know—' The wine waiter approached and Simon looked up at her.

'I hope you like wine with your meal. They do an excellent Mosel here.' When he had ordered and the waiter had gone he looked at her speculatively for a moment, then said quietly:

'Forgive me, Nicola. I didn't mean to cut you off like that.'

She shook her head. 'Of course not—I should have—'

'Please—' he interrupted. 'Before we go any further I owe you an explanation. I told you before that one of the reasons I was against you coming to Meadowlands had nothing to do with you personally. I realise now how unfair that must have sounded. That reason was that you belong to a past I'm trying hard to erase.'

Nicola looked miserably at her plate. 'It's all right. I quite understand.'

He smiled wryly. 'I don't think you do, but never mind. Maybe it's stupid to try anyway.'

She looked up at him tentatively. 'I think perhaps it is.' She bit her lip. 'They were happy times, weren't they? It seems sad to forget them.'

'Happy in the sense that ignorance is bliss. One can't go back, and if I could—' He broke off and she looked at him quickly.

'If it would help to talk—'

'No!' For a moment he looked at her almost

angrily, then he smiled—that same soul-melting smile she remembered so poignantly. 'What am I thinking of? I brought you here for a pleasant evening, not to depress you. Now, tell me what you think of the wine.'

The moment was gone. Nicola had the feeling that he had put up a barrier between them. Their relationship had improved, but she was no nearer to knowing him than before.

They made small talk through the rest of the meal, then walked outside to take their coffee on the terrace. The light was fading fast now and lights were twinkling in the small boats moored in the harbour. Across the bay the sea was smooth, a rippling irridescent green with tiny wavelets breaking on the narrow strip of sand at the foot of the sea wall. Behind them rose a steep, wooded hill with houses perched among the trees. Nicola watched as windows lit up one by one to glitter through the treetops. She sighed.

'This is a beautiful place.' She smiled wryly. 'It has Leeds beaten hollow.'

Simon shrugged. 'Cities have a special beauty of their own.' Again he gave her that speculative look. 'Was there any particular reason why you wanted to leave Leeds, Nicola?' he asked.

A mental picture of Chris saying goodbye flashed into her mind and out again. 'No—at least, only the one I told you about. I wanted to be more involved with the patients.'

'I warned you about becoming too personally involved.'

She nodded. 'I'm sure I can handle that.'

'I think perhaps you can,' he agreed. 'So there was nothing else—you weren't trying to escape?'

She looked up, frowning. 'Escape?'

'From a—relationship perhaps?'

She looked away. 'Oh—in a way, yes, that too. Though it was nothing serious.' She was puzzled. Why was he asking her these questions? A moment later he supplied the answer:

'Forgive me. I just wanted to be sure you would not change your mind and go rushing back to make up some lover's tiff. A stable relationship with your patients is an important part of the job at Meadowlands, you know.'

She felt the blood rush to her cheeks. What did he take her for? 'I *do* know,' she said stiffly. 'And you need have no fears on that score, I can assure you.' She shivered as a chill wind suddenly sprang up, ruffling the surface of the water and setting the boats in the harbour bobbing. 'I think I'd like to go now. I'm getting cold.'

'Of course—I'm sorry.'

As they sat side by side in the car Nicola watched the strong hands on the steering wheel and felt bleak. At times during the evening she had thought they were getting on well, then that curtain would come down between them again. Now they were back to square one—Simon polite and distant and she, as tongue-tied as ever.

As they drew up outside the Dower House he turned to her. 'Come in for a nightcap?'

She hesitated. 'I really should be getting back. I

told the Shelfords I wouldn't be late.'

'Just one wouldn't take long,' he said. 'The last time you were here we got off to a bad start—and you said you were cold. A drink will warm you up.'

This time they went in through the front door and Nicola found herself in a pleasant square hall with a pretty curved staircase. The floor was covered by a rose pink carpet and on the wall above the telephone table was a large framed print of Monet's 'Waterlily Pool'. Simon led the way through to the comfortable living room and helped her off with her coat, then he went to the sideboard and poured her a brandy.

One thing about the room surprised Nicola now that she had time to look round. There were no photographs of Claudia—none of her pictures either as far as she could tell. More Impressionist prints decorated the walls and there were two bookcases full of books. Had Simon put away all her things so that he wouldn't be reminded?

She took a sip of the brandy and felt its warmth seep into her veins.

He smiled at her. 'Warmer now? We can't have you catching cold because of me, can we? That would never do.' Although his words were light and friendly his eyes had that clouded abstracted look again and she felt that he was merely carrying out a duty—being a good host. Quickly she drank the rest of the brandy and got to her feet.

'That was very pleasant. Thank you, but I feel I mustn't take up any more of your time. You probably have a busy schedule tomorrow.' She had almost reached the door when it opened and a small slight figure stood on the threshold.

'Daddy—I heard—Oh!' Maria stared wide-eyed at Nicola. She wore a pair of pink pyjamas that were slightly too small for her, the sleeves and trousers too short for the fast growing arms and legs, and her long dark hair hung loose to her waist. Simon smiled and stepped forward.

'Now, young lady, why aren't you asleep? Back to bed with you. I'll come up a little later.'

Maria peered at Nicola, frowning a little in concentration, then the dark eyes lit up with recognition. 'I know you! You used to look after me when I was in the hospital having my appendix out. You were the one who used to make up the lovely stories! You're Nurse—Nurse—Page!'

'That's right. How clever of you to remember! You were a very little girl then and I was a very new nurse,' Nicola smiled.

The child's smile illuminated her serious little face, tinging her olive skin with a rosy pink flush. 'Have you come to be a nurse at Meadowlands? Shall I see you again? I hope so. I've got a dog. His name is Seamus.'

'I know, I've already met him.'

Simon intervened: 'Upstairs with you now. It's late, Nurse Page has to go and you should be asleep.'

'All right.' Maria turned at the door. 'Will you ask Nurse Page to come to tea, Daddy? I'd like to see her again. Goodnight.'

When the child had gone, running lightly up the

stairs like a small pink ghost. Nicola picked up her coat.

'I really must be going.'

'Of course.' As he helped her on with her coat his fingers brushed her neck briefly and she felt an involuntary shiver go through her. He felt it too.

'You're still cold!' His eyes looked questioningly into hers, but she shook her head.

'No—I'm fine now. Thank you for a lovely evening. Goodnight.'

'I'll walk across the park with you. It's late—and dark.'

'Please—I'm sure there's no need for you to bother.'

But he ignored her protests. As they crossed the stretch of parkland between the Dower House and Meadowlands he took her arm and at the rear door that led to her flat he stopped and looked down at her.

'It may perhaps surprise you to know that you are the first person my daughter has taken any interest in since—since the accident.'

Nicola looked at him. 'That's very flattering. I'm surprised she remembered someone from a time that must have been far from pleasant for her.'

'Perhaps it wasn't as unpleasant as you think,' he said softly. 'And perhaps Maria has a lesson for us. Maybe there are times when we should choose to walk back—to throw some light into the dark corners.' To her immense surprise he picked up one of her hands and brushed his lips lightly across the fingers.

'Thank you, Nicola. Goodnight.' And he was gone, leaving her staring after him through the darkness, a wistful longing in her heart.

CHAPTER FIVE

WHEN Nicola made her rounds the following morning her heart was light. She had wakened to the sun streaming through her window and the memory of the previous evening slowly filtered back into her mind, filling her heart with optimism. Much of what Simon had said remained a puzzle and she still didn't fully understand his sudden change of attitude towards her, but at least it was a start. As she put on her uniform she remembered his goodnight and the small sweet gesture that had quickened her heart. Then, before she could stop them, Laura's words echoed once again: 'You want him and the sooner you face the fact, the better!' She studied her reflection in the mirror as she pinned on her cap. Well—was there anything so terrible about being in love? she asked herself defensively. What she had felt for Simon had lasted four years and survived every possible opposition. Surely it was nothing to be ashamed of.

The morning was a busy one. Each of the patients had their own jobs to do in the training flat that was a feature of Meadowlands. Specially wide doors and ramps designed for wheelchairs led into rooms equipped with fittings built at the right height for seated workers. Here the patients accustomed themselves to the daily chores of looking

after themselves in a new environment. But Nicola
was rapidly learning that mere physical survival was
only the tip of the iceberg for these people. For
cases like Natalie and Gerry mental adjustment
was hardest, and she wanted desperately to help
them. Both must take up a new career in order to be
independent, but first they must face the hard fact
that their past life was gone for ever. This, she
understood, was hardest of all.

She helped the two paraplegics to rise and dress,
although they were both becoming adept at using
the special equipment in their rooms, then she
checked Frank. The arm he had lost was the left
one, but, unfortunately for him, he had been left-
handed. Today, he told her, it was his turn to cook a
meal. He was planning to make a bacon and egg pie
and a sponge pudding.

'My Maureen used to be a dab hand at a bacon
and egg pie,' he told her as he struggled into his
jacket. 'She always used to shoo me out of the
kitchen but I loved to watch her cook. I reckon I
picked up enough tips to keep me from starving.'
He looked at Nicola wistfully. 'What I dread most
about leaving here is the loneliness,' he confided.
'We were a close family, the three of us. I never was
much of a one for mixing with the lads at the
factory.'

'Have you been to see your old boss yet?' Nicola
asked him. 'Sister said that she thought he might be
willing to give you another job.'

Frank shook his head. 'I'm not going back there.
Maybe you think I'm proud but I couldn't stand the

looks of pity and I don't want to feel I'm a charity case.'

'I'm sure it wouldn't be like that,' Nicola assured him. 'But if there's something new you could take up—'

'There is!' he told her quickly. 'I've been helping Ted Shelford in the greenhouses and he reckons I manage pretty well. I've always liked pottering in the garden and it seems there's a college in Gloucestershire where I could take a course in horticulture. Sister says she'll get the Social Worker to look into it for me.'

'That's wonderful, Frank.'

'Yes.' He smiled. 'Something to look forward to—for the first time in ages.'

She left Frank's room feeling happy for him but when she went in to Natalie she found a very different picture confronting her. Standing by the window looking gloomily down into the garden, Natalie had made no attempt to get dressed. Nicola looked at her fob-watch and saw that it was ten-to-eight.

'Come along, Natalie. High time you were ready for breakfast. It's today that you're going into Medchester for the first of your new treatments, isn't it? You don't want to be late.'

Natalie turned to look at her, her eyes dull. 'I'm not going,' she said flatly.

'*Not*—but why?'

'I was watching a programme on TV last night. It was all about laser treatment and it said it could make scars worse!'

Nicola shook her head. 'Only in the hands of the wrong people. Lasers are like any other form of technical equipment—dangerous unless used by doctors and properly trained people. Surely you know that you couldn't be in better hands that Mr Grey's. If he says that laser treatment will help you then you can be sure it will.' She opened the wardrobe and began to take out Natalie's clothes. The girl didn't move.

'He only said it might.'

'Doctors are always cautious,' Nicola told her. 'Come on now. Please get dressed or you won't be ready when your transport arrives and you don't want to make everyone else late, do you?'

Natalie began to climb reluctantly and thoughtfully into her clothes. She turned to the mirror to comb her long dark hair, looking at Nicola through the glass. 'I'll go if you come with me,' she said suddenly.

Nicola looked up from tidying the girl's night-clothes away. If Natalie wanted her—felt more secure in her company—it was something of a breakthrough. How could she refuse?

'All right, I'll see what Sister says,' she promised. 'But if she can't spare me you will try to understand, won't you?'

Natalie nodded as the breakfast bell sounded. 'I'll understand, but I won't go.'

Nicola tapped on the door of Sister's office and went in. 'May I have a word, Sister?'

'Of course. Sit down.'

'It's Natalie. She says she won't go to the hospital

for her treatment unless I go with her. I think she's afraid—basically it's just someone to hold her hand,' Nicola explained.

Sister Martin smiled. 'Well done. It's a big step forward for Natalie to ask for help. Of course you must go. We have to be flexible here, unlike a hospital. Your duty is wherever you are needed most. If I might make a suggestion, it might be more diplomatic to go in "mufti".'

Nicola got up. 'Of course. I'll go and change at once. Thanks, Sister.'

'No, thank *you*, Staff. It seems you're getting through and that's what Meadowlands is all about.' She looked up with a smile. 'By the way—did you have a pleasant evening?'

Nicola stopped in the doorway. 'Yes, but—'

'I'm so glad. I dropped a hint to Mr Grey that I thought he'd been less than encouraging to you. I thought he might apologise but I must say I was surprised when I heard that he'd invited you out to dinner. His conscience *must* have been troubling him.'

'But how did you hear?' Nicola was taken aback.

Sister smiled. 'From Marjorie, who in turn heard from her friend, Maud Dickens who keeps house for the Greys.' She shook her head, chuckling over Nicola's incredulous expression. 'You're living in a village again now, my dear. Surely you haven't forgotten how the grapevine works?'

As she changed in her room Nicola fumed at her own naivety. Now she understood Simon's sudden change of attitude. What exactly had Sister Martin said to him? She winced with embarrassment. Why hadn't she kept her feelings to herself? All the time last night he had been humouring her! And she had been foolish enough to think—Oh! She gave an angry shrug and picked up her handbag, swinging out of the room. Well, she wouldn't make *that* mistake again!

The hospital minibus arrived on time with its collection of country patients going into Medchester General for various treatment. Nicola and Natalie sat at the back and Nicola noticed that the other girl had combed her hair forward over her forehead, letting the left side fall over her scarred cheek. She was developing a habit of drooping her head, as though to avoid the eyes of others. Nicola reached out to touch her arm.

'Cheer up. I understand there's hardly any sensation at all and it doesn't take long. Just think how wonderful it will be to see the scars fading. Before you know it you'll be back at work.'

'You must be joking,' Natalie said miserably. 'No one will employ me as a model again. Even the people I thought of as my friends have dropped me!'

Nicola thought about this for a moment. Perhaps it wasn't all that surprising. Natalie hadn't been an easy person to be with since her accident. For her friends in the modelling world it would be painfully difficult to know how to approach her.

'Was there anyone special?' she probed gently.

Natalie looked up, her large brown eyes misty.

'Yes—his name was Rick Milton. He's a photographer and making quite a name for himself. He and I were—close. There was a misunderstanding between us on the night it happened. He thought I was out with someone else. I broke a date with him you see.'

'And you weren't?'

'Yes—but not in the way he thought. It was a job—a chance of one at least. I was offered a contract with one of the largest mail-order firms in the country. I couldn't pass it up.'

'I see. What happened?'

The girl drew a deep breath. 'We were dining at a smart restaurant in Mayfair. We were in the basement where there was a small dance floor. No one knew how the fire started and by the time we knew about it the staircase was ablaze. There was a fire exit, of course, but everyone panicked and there was a terrible crush. I fell and my face was pressed against the metal rail of the staircase.'

Nicola squeezed her hand. 'It must have been horrible. But you will be all right again, you know.' Suddenly an idea struck her. 'I have heard of people who model just their hands, their legs or their hair. You might do that until your face is completely healed.'

'It's no use kidding myself,' Natalie said disconsolately. 'No one will ever want to look at me again. I'd just be an embarrassment.'

But an idea was forming in the back of Nicola's mind. Rick Milton—that was the name Natalie had mentioned. Obviously there had been a misunderstanding between them. It would do no harm to have a word with him.

Medchester General was a large modern hospital and the various outpatients' clinics opened off a wide central corridor. As they settled down in the waiting area Nicola turned to Natalie.

'There's ten minutes to go till your appointment. Would you like a coffee?'

Natalie nodded. 'I'd love one.'

Nicola went back down the corridor to the machine and put her money in but just as she was turning back she almost collided with a tall white-coated figure. 'Oh—sorry!' Her eyes swept upwards and she gave a cry of surprise as she saw who it was.

'Oh, it's you—but I thought you were taking the clinic this morning.' She glanced towards the other end of the corridor where Natalie was nervously waiting.

Simon smiled. 'So I am, but I've just been called up to the ward on an emergency. Have you come with Natalie?'

'Yes.' She remembered her conversation with Sister Martin that morning and lowered her eyes. 'I'd—better get back to her before this coffee gets cold.'

He stopped her with a hand on her arm. 'Maria was talking about you again this morning at breakfast. She made me promise to ask you to tea. It's quite lucky, running into you like this.'

'You've been more than generous already. There's no need to do any more,' she told him, her eyes flashing. 'I've no idea what Sister said to you but I'm not as thin-skinned as all that!' And without waiting for his reaction she hurried away down the corridor, leaving Simon staring after her.

There was a slight delay, owing to Simon having been called away, but as soon as Natalie was called in for her treatment Nicola made her way towards the row of telephone kiosks in the reception hall. With the help of Directory Enquiries she got the number she wanted and dialled it, hoping that Rick Milton would be in. She was in luck, after a few rings the telephone was answered by a deep male voice:

'Rick Milton here. Can I help you?'

'Ah—you don't know me but I'm a friend of Natalie Friar,' Nicola told him. 'You know, I suppose, that she is recovering from severe burns?'

'Yes—I did know that,' the voice said noncommitally.

'Well, she is at Meadowlands Rehabilitation Centre in the New Forest,' Nicola told him. 'It's just outside a village called Farthingbridge. She's been very badly shaken by her injuries, Mr Milton. As you probably know she has no close family or relatives and she can use all the help she can get just now. She mentioned your name to me and I happen to know that a visit from you would mean a lot to her—but she has no idea I'm ringing you so it will be entirely up to you.'

There was a long silence and for a moment she thought he might have hung up, then he said:

'The New Forest, you said? Give me that address again, will you?'

Hopes rising, she repeated the address.

'How is she—how are the burns?' he asked.

'Healing well—it's her confidence that is taking time,' Nicola told him.

'Yes—well—I can't promise anything but I'll see what I can do. You'll have to excuse me now. I have a photographic session in progress.' And a moment later she found herself listening to the dialling tone. Obviously Mr Milton didn't believe in wasting time in pleasantries! She hung up the receiver and walked thoughtfully back to the clinic, hoping she had done the right thing.

Natalie came out looking more cheerful than she had for a long time and on the way back to Meadowlands in the minibus it was she who did all the talking whilst Nicola sat wrapped in her own thoughts.

That evening the time hung heavily for Nicola. Strictly speaking she was off duty after the patients' supper but often she stayed with them longer if she wasn't going out, either watching the television or sharing some other form of recreation with them. This evening she had gone straight to her flat. But after an hour of her own company she could bear it no longer and went downstairs to the kitchen to look for Marjorie. She found her blanching vegetables for the freezer.

'Would you like a coffee if I make it for you?' she asked. Marjorie looked up with a grateful smile.

'Wouldn't I just! My Ted is the best gardener for

miles around but there are times when I wish he wasn't quite so successful!' She nodded towards the pile of beans and sweetcorn awaiting her attention on the table. 'Look at that lot. I'll be up till midnight at this rate!'

Nicola smiled. 'But think of the work it'll save you later. No wondering what to cook in the winter—no preparation.'

Marjorie pushed a strand of hair out of her eyes. 'Mmm—all I can think of at this moment is how much my legs ache!'

But Marjorie's mind proved to have more than one track as she sat down opposite Nicola and eyed her with interest over the coffee cups. 'A little bird tells me you were off gadding last night,' she said archly. 'Ah—I'm glad the Doctor had some attractive feminine company. It's just what he needs.' She peered hopefully at Nicola. 'Did you go somewhere nice then?'

Nicola shrugged, trying hard not to feel irritated. 'Quite nice, thank you. Mr Grey took me out for a meal. Apparently he felt he'd been rather short with me and wanted to make amends.'

Marjorie nodded. 'Yes, that sounds like him—generous to a fault. My friend Maud is always telling me what a good employer he is.' She leaned across the table, lowering her voice although there was no one else to hear. 'Maybe I shouldn't be telling you this, but she said he was a different man this morning. *Singing* in his bath, he was! You must have cheered him up and no mistake. That's nice to know, now, isn't it?'

'Wonderful,' Nicola said without enthusiasm.

'And to think that child remembered you from all those years ago. Now that really *is* something!'

Nicola got to her feet. It seemed Maud Dickens had spared Marjorie nothing of the previous evening's happenings. She began to wonder if she could have been hiding under the table at the Harbour Club!

'Look at poor Betsy!' she said, desperate to change the subject. 'She looks really miserable. I'll take her for a walk, shall I?' And she reached down Betsy's collar and lead from behind the door and began to fasten them round the startled animal's neck while Marjorie stared in surprise.

'Well, she's been for a walk actually, dear,' she said. 'Ted took her just after tea, but if you want—' She broke off as Nicola and the little dog disappeared out through the kitchen door. 'Well—' she muttered to herself. 'You'd think she'd be tired after a long day!'

Nicola took off at a brisk pace, going down the drive towards the road. She would not go across the park again, by the Dower House. Tonight she had no wish to run into Simon. Betsy followed on her lead, delighted if surprised at the unexpected extra walk. They reached the main gate and turned right towards the village, but they had not gone more than a hundred yards when a car approached, coming in the opposite direction and Nicola saw with dismay that it was Simon's dark blue saloon. She picked Betsy up and stood well into the grass verge, hoping that she would not be noticed. The car passed and she drew a sigh of relief, then it stopped and began to reverse. Simon wound down the window

'Nicola!'

She turned to look at him. 'Oh—hello,' she said with a feeble effort at feigning surprise.

He reached across to open the door. 'Get into the car for a moment. I want to talk to you.'

She bit her lip. 'I was taking the dog for a walk.'

'Please—do as I say!'

Something about his commanding tone made her obey, but as she slid into the passenger seat beside him she felt like an erring schoolgirl, summoned to the headmistress's study, and she resented the fact. Determined not to make it easy for him to admonish her she said nothing, but looked him straight in the eye.

'Perhaps you'd care to expand on the remarks you made to me at the hospital this morning,' he said coolly.

Her eyes slid away from his face. 'I—I'm not fond of being patronised,' she said unhappily. 'Anything I said to Sister Martin was not meant as a complaint, and certainly not meant to—to—'

'Sister Martin and I are old friends,' he interrupted. 'In my early days she always let me know in no uncertain terms when she thought I was wrong and nothing has changed between us. I still respect her opinions. It's true that she hinted to me that I'd been unfair to you but that had nothing to do with my taking you out to dinner last night.'

She made no reply. Sick with embarrassment she

sat staring down at her hands. Suddenly he reached out to touch her cheek. 'Nicola—we were friends—colleagues once. I wanted to resume that. Is that being patronising?' It's a long time since I allowed myself any social life. I'm out of practice as I told you—especially with the opposite sex. But it's time Maria and I started to live again. Will you help us?'

She looked up at him in surprise. 'Why me?'

'You can't know the importance of what happened last night,' he explained. 'For the past two years Maria has gone through life like a little machine. She's taken no real interest in anything. Oh, she's done her schoolwork and her behaviour has been perfect—*too* perfect. She's been like a mechanical doll, going through the motions of living without any sign of emotion. She has no friends, no hobbies, no likes or dislikes. Once she was a normal, mischievous little girl but after the accident it was as though something inside her turned to ice.'

'She must miss her mother terribly,' Nicola said.

Simon went on: 'Last night, when she saw you she seemed to come to life again. You can't know what that meant to me, Nicola. To see interest in her eyes again. She made me promise to ask you to tea. You will come, won't you?'

She swallowed hard. It would be churlish to refuse a request like that, yet disappointment swamped her.

'Of course I'll be glad to come if you really think it will help Maria,' she said bleakly.

He looked at her searchingly. 'I don't want you to think I'm simply using you, Nicola. Believe me, it isn't like that. I want you to come too.' He cupped her chin and turned her face until he could look into her eyes. 'I admit that I wanted to forget my time at Bishop's Wood,' he told her quietly. 'I thought that anything or anyone from those days would be like a ghost from the past—would haunt me in a way I didn't want to be haunted. But now I see that isn't true.' His eyes as they looked into hers were grave and serious. 'You're like a sweet breath of spring in a long cold winter, Nicola. Don't deny me that small delight.'

She looked up at him, his eyes holding hers for a long moment. Was she dreaming or had he actually said those words to her? 'I'll come on my next day off,' she whispered.

He bent his head to brush his lips across hers. 'Thank you. It means a great deal to me.'

She stood by the roadside, watching until the red tail light of his car was swallowed up in the dusk, her head still reeling and her lips still tingling from their brief contact with his. At that moment she would have followed him to the North Pole if he had asked her to. Laura would have laughed and called her a fool—maybe she was. All Nicola knew was that she couldn't wait for her next day off.

But a few days later something happened that almost put Simon out of her mind—something that was to have far-reaching effects on more than one person at Meadowlands.

CHAPTER SIX

WHEN the scarlet sports car drew up outside the front entrance of Meadowlands that afternoon it caused quite a stir, as did its occupant: a tall good-looking young man dressed in expensive looking, trendy clothes. Nicola was working in Sister Martin's office when one of the care assistants tapped on the door.

'Staff, there's a visitor for Miss Friar. Will you see him?'

Nicola came out into the hall where the man was waiting. 'Good afternoon, you wanted to see Natalie?' she asked.

He looked her up and down. 'Are you the Matron or whatever it's called?'

'No, it's Sister Martin's day off today. I'm Staff Nurse Page.'

'I see. I got this phone call the other day—'

At once she realised who he was. 'Ah—you must be Mr Milton. It was I who rang you.' She held out her hand and Rick Milton shook it briefly.

'Well, can I see Natalie?' he asked. 'You didn't say when the visiting times were so I just hoped it would be okay.'

'We don't have visiting times here. Friends are welcome at any time within reason. Please come into the lounge. I'll go and see if I can find Natalie.'

Nicola went in search of Natalie, feeling a little apprehensive. If only Rick Milton had telephoned to warn that he was coming. Suppose Natalie refused to see him? What on earth would she say to him? Natalie had been to the hospital for treatment that morning and was resting in her room. When Nicola put her head round the door she found to her relief that the girl was not sleeping but reading a book. She looked up in surprise.

'Natalie—you have a visitor.'

Natalie's eyes opened wide as she sat up. 'A visitor? Who? No one knows I'm here.'

'Someone does.' Nicola sat on the edge of the bed. 'Now look—don't panic, but a few days ago I rang your friend, Rick Milton. It's him.'

'You rang Rick?' Natalie sprang up from the bed. 'How *could* you?' she shouted. 'I can't possibly let him see me like this!'

'Yes you can,' Nicola said firmly, standing behind her at the mirror. 'Take an honest look at yourself, Natalie. Your face is improving daily now. It's heaps better than when I first came here. You have to start facing people again. You can't stay here forever.' Through the mirror she saw the large dark eyes fill with tears and pity wrung her heart.

'You don't know what it's like,' Natalie said brokenly. 'All I've ever had is my looks. I'm not clever and dedicated like you. I feel like a—a crushed flower—only fit for the rubbish heap. When Rick sees me he'll—' She covered her face with her hands. 'Oh I couldn't bear to see his eyes when he looks at me!'

Nicola grasped her shoulders and turned her gently towards her. 'When he looks at you he'll see the same you he's always seen,' she said firmly. 'Except for the smile. Come on now, why don't you comb your hair and put on a little lipstick, then come down. I'll talk to him while he's waiting, eh?'

Natalie hesitated. 'Do you really think I should?'

'Yes, I do. After all he's driven an awfully long way to see you. He wouldn't do that if he didn't care about you, would he?'

Nicola crossed her fingers as she went back down the stairs. Maybe today would be a turning point for Natalie. All she really needed was for someone to prove to her that she had always been more than just a collection of perfect features.

'She's coming in a moment,' she told Rick Milton. 'Sorry to keep you waiting but she was resting. She went to the hospital for treatment this morning you see.'

He looked up with a smile. 'That's all right, there's no hurry. What kind of treatment is she having?'

'Laser treatment. It's something comparatively new.'

He looked interested. 'Yes—I've heard of it. Tell me, what exactly does it do?'

Nicola sat down. 'Well, in cases like Natalie's it helps to increase the supply of blood to the area of the burn, which helps it heal faster—at least, that is the simple explanation.'

He smiled at her wryly. 'I *am* quite intelligent,'

he told her. 'I can understand words of more than two syllables, if you speak *very* slowly of course.'

She blushed at his sarcasm. 'Of course, I wasn't—I mean, some people don't like a lot of details. The laser—by increasing the supply of blood, helps in the building of new collagen and elastin fibres, which are what gives the skin its suppleness. It isn't very complicated really.'

He laughed. 'There, you see, I actually understood. I'm not as stupid as I look.' He shook his head at her. 'I'm sorry, I'm embarrassing you. I didn't mean to tease.'

Nicola was relieved when the door opened at that moment and Natalie came in. She slipped out quietly, closing the door behind her with a sigh. Rick didn't seem to her the easiest person to be with. She only hoped that he would be kinder to Natalie.

Half an hour later she heard the roar of a car engine and, looking out of the office window she saw Rick Milton's car heading off down the drive with Natalie in the passenger seat. Obviously he was taking her out for tea. It looked as though the visit was a success. Nicola gave a sigh of relief. Her work here at Meadowlands could be very rewarding at times.

It was almost suppertime when Natalie reappeared. She tapped on the door of the office and when Nicola called for her to come in she was amazed at the change in her. A couple of hours with Rick had worked a magic that even the laser couldn't bring about.

'Would it be all right if I went up to London the day after tomorrow?' Natalie asked, her eyes glowing with excitement.

'I don't see why not,' Nicola smiled. 'I take it the visit was a success?'

Natalie smiled happily. 'Yes—Rick didn't seem to see my scars at all. He wants me to go up to his studio for some tests. He even hinted that he may be able to get me a modelling job again quite soon.'

'That's wonderful news, Natalie. I'll check with Sister, but I'm sure it'll be all right as long as you're happy about it.' She glanced at her watch. 'You'd better hurry now. The supper bell will be going any minute.'

'I'm far too excited to eat!' Natalie turned at the door. 'Thanks—for all you've done. I didn't believe you but I can see now that you were right.'

Natalie's trip to London coincided with Nicola's next day off—the day she had been invited to tea with Simon and Maria. In the morning she had planned to go into Medchester to do some shopping and travelled in with Natalie on the bus. The girl looked happy and excited. Her hair was freshly shampooed and styled and she wore one of the glamorous outfits she had not worn since her accident. She chattered all the way about her old life and the friends she hoped to contact on her brief visit. Nicola went with her to the station and saw her off on the train, then turned her footsteps towards the town.

After buying sweets for Maria and collecting some small items the other patients at Meadowlands had asked for she had her hair done and treated herself to lunch at a small restaurant by the river, then she caught the bus back in plenty of time to change.

She chose a dress of pale green linen and paid special attention to her make-up before walking across the park to the Dower House. The door was opened to her by Maud Dickens, Simon's housekeeper, who looked her over with obvious interest.

'I've heard so much about you from my friend Marjorie,' she said. 'It's nice to meet you at last.' She led the way through the hall. 'Mr Grey has had to go out on an urgent call, I'm afraid, but Maria is waiting for you in the garden. She thought it might be nice to have your tea out there.' She opened the living room door where the french windows stood open. 'All of a twitter she's been, looking forward to you coming,' Maud confided. 'You wouldn't believe the fuss and bother over what we should have for tea.'

'I do hope you haven't been put to a lot of trouble,' Nicola said. Her heart had turned a sommersault of disappointment at the news that Simon would not be with them. Maud smiled and shook her head.

'Nothing is too much trouble to see her as involved as this,' she said. 'It's such a treat to see her interested in something again—playing hostess. Well, I'll leave you to join her. I'll bring out the tea in a moment.'

On the lawn a low table had been set out with three chairs in the shade of the mulberry tree.

Maria sat in one of them, the dog, Seamus at her feet. When she saw Nicola coming she jumped up and came to meet her.

'Oh, you're here. I'm so pleased you could come. This is Seamus. He's an Irish Wolfhound.'

Nicola stroked the shaggy head. 'He's lovely, but a bit scary. I met him before, on the first night I was here. I thought he was going to eat poor little Betsy, Mrs Shelford's dog.'

'He'd never do that, though he does like to play,' Maria told her gravely.

Nicola gave her the small parcel she carried. 'Here, I seem to remember that you like these.'

Maria unwrapped the parcel eagerly and found a box of peppermint creams. She smiled up at Nicola.

'Lovely, yes I do like them, but so does Daddy. I shall have to hide them!'

All through tea Maria chattered, recalling her stay in the children's ward of Bishop's Wood Hospital with startling clarity as though it had been a memorable experience rather than a traumatic one. Nicola found herself warming to the child. There was something heart-rendingly vulnerable about her as she sat there on the grass, her long legs tucked under her and her arm around the neck of the dog. Odd that a child as privileged as she had no happier memory than a stay in hospital.

At last, reluctant to outstay her welcome, Nicola got to her feet. 'It's getting late. I think I should be going now, Maria.'

The child's face fell. 'Oh—but Daddy isn't home yet. Do stay till he comes.'

But Nicola shook her head. 'I'll see you again another day. When your father gets home he'll be tired and hungry. He won't expect to find me still here.'

'That's not true. I was hoping to make it before you left.'

His voice startled her and she swung round to see him standing in the open doorway. 'Oh—hello. I didn't know—'

He walked towards them. 'Is there any tea left in that pot, or have you two drunk it all?' He smiled at Maria. 'Well, have you had a nice afternoon?'

'Yes, thank you, Daddy. You will make Nicola come again, won't you?' The brown velvet eyes looked up at him imploringly.

Simon laughed. 'I can't *make* her do anything, Maria. We'll just have to hope that she likes us well enough to want to come.' He looked at Nicola as he spoke and she felt her cheeks colouring. To hide her embarrassment she looked again at her watch.

'I really must go now. I half promised to go over to Milton Green,' she said impulsively.

Simon nodded. 'I'll drive you down to the village. I promised a colleague I'd look in at a patient at the hospital and I might as well go now as later.' He looked at Maria. 'We mustn't monopolise Nicola. She has her own family, you know.'

'Have you?' Maria looked up at her. 'You didn't tell me anything about them. Have you lots of brothers and sisters?'

'Just one brother, but I don't see him very often,' Nicola told her. 'He teaches music and makes his own musical instruments. He teaches some of his pupils to make them too.'

Maria looked thoughtful. 'What's his name?'

'Terry. He has a sort of travelling workshop which he takes from place to place.' She laughed. 'It's a good job he isn't married. No wife would ever stand his kind of life for long.'

They said goodbye and Simon accompanied her out to his car. When they were out of sight of the house he said: 'This brother of yours—he sounds a very interesting man. Do you think he might find time to come down to Meadowlands? We're always looking for craftsmen who will come and talk to the patients—give them new ideas—and what he does sounds fascinating.'

'I'm sure he'd be delighted to come,' Nicola told him. 'He's done some remarkable work with disturbed children and disabled people. He seems to have a special flair, though he isn't a qualified teacher and his methods are rather unorthodox. He lives a precarious existence, relying on private engagements and earning money by playing at concerts and lecturing about his unusual instruments.'

'Will you contact him and see when he's free?' Simon asked.

'I certainly will.' She smiled. 'Laura will be pleased. She's been trying to get him to come down for a visit for ages. This time he'll have no excuse.'

They were nearing the village when he turned to her with a frown. 'What bus were you planning to catch? The five-thirty will have gone and there isn't another for an hour and a half.'

Nicola bit her lip. 'I know—but it doesn't matter.' He was looking at her closely and she added: 'Actually I wasn't really going—I just didn't want to outstay my welcome.'

He stopped the car and turned to her. 'You mean you'd have let me drop you at the bus stop, then calmly walked back to Meadowlands?'

She shrugged. 'It's a pleasant enough evening.'

'If you have no other plans why don't you come with me?' he asked suddenly 'It's Bishop's Wood Hospital I'm going to—the Intensive Care Unit. You might find some of your old friends still there. Well—would you like to?' He grinned at her wryly. 'If the answer's no, please don't feel you have to make any more excuses—just say.'

She smiled. 'I don't have to. I'd love to come. Thank you.'

On the way he told her that the patient was the victim of a car accident that morning on the motorway. 'As well as her other injuries she has severe facial lacerations,' he explained. 'When she is sufficiently recovered she will need further surgery to save her looks, which is where I come in. Fortunately she has a loving family to help and support her, unlike poor Natalie.'

'Natalie had a visit from an old boyfriend the other day,' she told him. 'And today she's gone up to London to meet him. He's a photographer and he's going to do some tests on her. She's so excited to think that she may soon be working again.'

He looked at her doubtfully. 'Well, that's good

news, of course, but I wouldn't really have thought she was ready for it yet.'

'There are other kinds of modelling—where only the legs, the feet or the hands are used,' she told him. 'I daresay they'll be tests for that, then later, when her face was healed—'

'That's a clever idea. I would never have thought of that.' He smiled at her and she felt a glow of satisfaction and pleasure. Maybe she was at last convincing him that she had a flair for this kind of work.

The Sister on Intensive Care had been at Bishop's Wood at the same time as Nicola, who watched through the glass panel of the ward door as she and Simon, gowned and masked, examined the patient. She glanced round at the familiar equipment—the monitors and ventilators she had grown so used to working with—and sighed wistfully. Here everything was so routine—so completely different from her new job at Meadowlands. Working in Intensive Care she had never had to make any monumental decisions. There had always been someone else to take that responsibility. In helping patients to readjust to a new life she suddenly saw that one wrong word could do infinite damage. For a fleeting instant she recalled Natalie's radiant face as she boarded the train this morning and for a moment she knew a moment of unease. Suppose Rick let her down? She pushed the thought from her. Surely he wouldn't have gone to the trouble he had if he didn't care for her?

They had coffee and a chat about old times in

Sister's office, then went down to the car park again. Simon looked enquiringly at her.

'Something to eat?'

She shook her head. 'You must be wanting to get home.'

He closed the car door. 'Sometimes home can be a lonely place.' He turned to her. 'It was marvellous to see Maria's response to you this afternoon and I promised to ask you to repeat the visit. You will, won't you?'

Nicola looked down at her hands. Coming back here to Bishop's Wood had brought back painfully poignant memories. Was she simply inviting all the heartache back again? Did Simon want her company simply for the sake of Maria? As though he read her thoughts he touched her arm.

'Nicola—the other evening you asked me if I wanted to talk. Are you still willing to listen?'

As she looked up at him she tried hard to keep the panic out of her eyes. Could she bear to sit and listen to him talking about Claudia—telling with his eyes how much he still loved and missed her? She should never have come to Meadowlands. She should have put this man out of her heart and mind long ago. But, as their eyes met, she knew hopelessly that she would listen for as long as he wanted to talk—that if there was the slightest chance of being with him, of being in the smallest way necessary to him, she would be here.

'If it will help, of course I am,' she said softly.

'Bless you.' Swiftly he bent and kissed her cheek,

then started the car. 'Not here—we'll find a quiet little place to eat.'

Nicola was silent as they drove. From time to time she glanced at the strong profile, wondering what went on inside Simon's mind. He seemed to have very little social life now. In the old days he and Claudia had been well known for the parties they had given, Nicola had even been to one or two herself. She remembered seeing them dancing together, Simon's eyes laughing down into his wife's lovely face. They had been the envy of everyone who knew them—not least her. Now he seemed to live only for his work, his daughter and Meadowlands. Maybe he felt an affinity with the patients there—disabled himself by his grief. As he concentrated on driving his mouth and jaw were tense, but as they drew up outside a tiny thatched inn she saw his mouth relax again into a smile.

All through the meal she waited for him to begin but it wasn't until they were drinking their coffee that he leaned forward and said:

'Nicola, just what have you heard—about Claudia's death?'

She looked at him. 'Only that there was a tragic accident—a car crash.'

His eyes held hers. 'That is all anyone knows, as far as I'm aware, though I've often wondered whether some people might suspect that there was more to it.'

Her eyes widened. 'More?'

He nodded. 'To all outward appearances we were the ideal couple. What no one knows is that on the night that Claudia was killed she was leaving me.'

The breath caught in her throat and her eyes held his for a long moment before she whispered: 'Oh Simon, I'm so sorry.'

He picked up his brandy glass and swirled the golden liquid thoughtfully. 'Unfortunately, it seems she had decided to take Maria with her, so she was involved in the crash too.' He took a deep breath and straightened his shoulders. 'I blame myself, of course. After my consultancy life changed for us. Claudia thought it would give me more free time, which I suppose it might well have done. But it didn't work that way. I was so involved—more so than ever before. Ambition to be at the top of my profession made me into a tenth-rate husband and father.'

'I can't believe that,' Nicola said.

He put down the glass and reached out to take her hand. 'I'm afraid it's true, nevertheless. It's a hard truth I've had to live with for the past two years, but since—' He looked round, then back at her. 'Let's get away from here. It's getting crowded.'

She stood up and he slipped her coat round her shoulders. She was acutely aware of the warmth of his hand on her arm and the intensity of the grey eyes that looked down into hers. Why was he telling her all this? Her heart skipped a beat and she dared not acknowledge the direction of her winging thoughts. He needed a friend, she told herself levelly. And she had promised herself to help him

in any way she could. If she were to be hurt in the
process then she would just have to cope with it.

They drove for some twenty minutes through the
fading light and when the car came to a halt again
she saw that they were at the top of a hill. Simon got
out and came round to her side of the car to open
the door for her. As she stood up she saw below
them the panoramic spread of the bay and harbour,
alive with hundreds of twinkling lights. The hillside
was crowded with tall pines which gave their fragrant breath to the evening air and a rising moon cast
inky shadows at their feet. Nicola sighed.

'Oh, how beautiful.'

'It's still warm,' Simon said. 'Shall we sit for a
while and enjoy the view?'

He took her hand and they sat together on the
grassy slope looking out over the treetops to a sea
like black rippled silk. After a moment Simon said:

'It was a shock, you know—seeing you again that
day at the interview. To begin with all I wanted to
do was to get you out of sight and mind again as
soon as I could. You reminded me, you see, of all
the happiness I threw away. In other words, I
suppose, of my failure as a person.' He looked at
her. 'Do you understand what it is I'm trying to say,
Nicola?'

She nodded. 'I—think so.'

'I was wrong,' he went on. 'Wrong and unfair to
you. Am I forgiven?'

'Please—' she shook her head. 'There's nothing
to forgive.' On impulse she reached out to put her
hand in his and immediately felt the long sensitive

fingers curl warmly round hers. Her heart quickening she looked up at him. He touched her cheek,
then, cupping her chin he drew her slowly towards
him. His lips brushed hers, then he drew her close
and kissed her deeply.

Nicola's head swam. How many times had she
dreamed of a moment such as this? Perhaps she was
dreaming even now. As his lips left hers she opened
her eyes and looked up at him.

'You're so sweet, Nicola,' he murmured huskily.
'So very sweet.'

She said nothing, happy just to be here in his
arms, nestling close to him, feeling the steady beat
of his heart against hers. After a moment his lips
found hers again and her arms crept round his neck,
her fingers entwining in the thick hair at the base of
his neck. His arms pulled her closer and she heard
him draw in his breath sharply as his lips hardened
against hers, demanding surrender. Slowly they
sank back together against the mossy turf and she
sighed tremulously. Simon's eyes burned into hers
as he stroked the soft blonde curls back from her
forehead, trailing his fingers down her cheek and
neck, softly caressing the hollow of her throat and
coming to rest on the silky curve of her breast. She
felt a sharp thrill of excitement as he slowly began
to unfasten the buttons of her dress, his eyes holding hers in mute appeal. As though in answer to
their smouldering question she reached up to draw
his head down to hers, finding his lips and allowing
her own to part beneath them, sliding her arms
inside his jacket to hold him close, thrilling to the

warmth and hardness of his strong back. For a long moment they lay entwined, caressing, mouths joining and re-joining, immersed totally in one another. For Nicola it was commitment. There was no going back now. Even if the moment proved only to be an impulse on Simon's part she would see it through. She closed her eyes, in her mind already giving herself—no thought of yesterday or tomorrow—only now, this moment—here with Simon in this beautiful place. She asked for nothing more.

'Nicola, darling—' His voice was soft and husky.

'Mmm?' She opened her eyes to look up at him, drowsy with love—dizzy with longing.

'Darling, I want you so much, but not here—not like this. Nicola, marry me.'

Her eyes slowly opened wide as his words sank into her numbed brain. She *must* be dreaming. Any moment now her alarm clock would ring and she would wake in her room at Meadowlands. She smiled and reached up to stroke his face.

'It's the moonlight talking. You don't really know me, Simon, in spite of all the years.'

He bent to kiss her swiftly. 'I know all I need to know,' he whispered. 'I know that you're young and sweet—and that I need you badly.'

She brushed her cheek against his. 'I need you too, Simon—I always have—ever since the very first time I saw you—when I had no business to think of you like that.' There—she had admitted it. What Laura had said had been true and suddenly it didn't seem to matter. Anyway what did it matter what one said in a dream? 'There's no one here but us,' she whispered against his ear. 'We're alone and if you want me—' She pressed close to him and heard again his sharply indrawn breath. For a moment they clung desperately to each other and she felt a shudder of anticipation ripple through her. She closed her eyes, the breath fluttering in her throat. Then suddenly Simon took her shoulders and held her away from him, looking searchingly into her eyes.

'Nicola, will you answer the question I asked you?'

She came down to earth with a bump. This wasn't a dream. It was real—so real that Simon was thinking about their professional relationship. If anyone were to discover them like this—even *hear* about it—it would not look good for him; especially when he had publicly opposed her appointment at Meadowlands. It might look as though there had been something between them in the past—when he was still married. She bit her lip, the warmth and magic of the evening suddenly gone.

'I think we should both have time to think about it,' she said haltingly. 'I'm afraid that in the cold light of day you may regret asking me.'

He let her go. 'I can see that it may seem sudden and impulsive to you, but I promise you it isn't, Nicola. When will you let me have your answer?'

'Soon.' There was a lump in her throat. This should be the happiest moment of her life, yet she felt oddly let down. Claudia would always be there between them—between her and her happiness. If only Simon had made love to her she would have said yes to his proposal joyfully, without another thought, but the mere fact that he had been able to hold back, to consider the mundane aspect—'I need you,' he had said. 'I want you.' But never 'I love you.'

She sat up and tidied herself, feeling suddenly cheap and shabby—awkward and sickeningly disappointed. 'It's getting late,' she said bleakly.

He helped her to her feet. 'Of course. I'll take you home.'

When he stopped the car outside the gates of Meadowlands he switched off the engine and turned to pull her close. When his lips touched hers again her heart ached so much that she almost cried out and she held herself rigidly unyielding in his arms, sick with the fear that she might reveal her feelings again. He looked into her eyes and in the dimness of the car's interior she could see their candour.

'I meant what I said, Nicola,' he said softly. 'It may have seemed to you like an impulse but I assure you it wasn't. I'm not given to impulses any more.'

With all her heart she longed to tell him how much she wished he was. Instead she said: 'I realise that. I'll give you my answer as soon as I can.'

As she began to get out of the car he said: 'Nicola—you won't let this keep you away, will you?' She turned to look at him, hope rising again inside her, then he added: 'Maria would never forgive me if I were the cause of her losing the lovely friend she has rediscovered.'

'Oh—no, of course.' She bent to look at him through the car window. 'You can tell Maria I'll see her soon again.' Then she turned and walked up the drive without a backward look.

CHAPTER SEVEN

'BUT you don't understand, Laura; I *want* to marry him!' Nicola sat facing her cousin across the kitchen table. She had asked Sister Martin for a few hours off and caught the late afternoon bus over to Milton Green on the day following Simon's proposal, unable to bear the agony of indecision any longer. Laura looked up at her despairingly.

'Oh, for heaven's sake, Nicola, grow up!' she said exasperatedly. 'Can't you see what you're doing to yourself? Why do you have to be so intense about it? Get him out of your system—*sleep* with him if that's what it takes!'

Nicola's head jerked up to look at her cousin in shocked surprise. 'Laura!' Then she lowered her eyes and added miserably: 'Don't think I wasn't willing to. That was when Simon proposed. I suppose he got carried away and felt he should do the decent thing.' She swallowed hard. 'That's what makes it so awful.'

Laura gave an exasperated sigh and rose to fill the kettle. 'Oh dear. It's worse than I thought.' She turned and looked at Nicola sitting there at the table with her arms folded and her shoulders slumped. 'Can't you see that you're making a complete fool of yourself, child? Heavens above, you're young and pretty. You should be having a good time, enjoying life, yet here you are mooning over a man years older than you who's obviously still in love with the wife he lost.'

Nicola's eyes filled with tears. 'If that's true why has he taken me out and—and behaved as he has?'

Laura threw up her hands. 'Because he couldn't help himself, of course. He's still a man after all and what man wouldn't be flattered by the admiration of a charming young woman like you? What did you expect?'

Nicola gave a shuddering sigh. 'So you agree then—that he only asked me to marry him because of Maria. Because she likes me and he thinks I'd be good for her?' Tears of despair ran down her cheeks and Laura crossed the kitchen to gather her into her sturdy arms.

'Oh don't look like that, honey. I can't bear to see you hurt any more now than I could when you were little. Let him go, love. You deserve better. When you marry you're going to be the most important person in your husband's life not just a substitute—a second best.' She took out a large handkerchief and began to wipe Nicola's face with it. 'Get out and have some fun before you get to be an old fogey like me. I hate to see you wasting your youth.'

'I don't think I know how to, Laura,' Nicola whispered.

'Buy yourself a little car,' Laura said impulsively. 'If you haven't got enough money I'll lend you some. After all you could do with your own transport with the local bus service being so infrequent.

It would help you to have a better social life. You could go sailing or swimming on your days off, there are plenty of clubs you could join. Or if you prefer village life there's church work—the vicar is always looking for people to run the youth club.' She shook Nicola gently. 'For heaven's sake, girl, surely you don't need *me* to tell you what to do with your free time!'

Nicola smiled, cheering up a little. Laura's down-to-earth common sense could usually put things into perspective for her. 'I was thinking of asking Terry to come down to Meadowlands to give a talk and demonstration of his craft and maybe an evening's entertainment,' she said.

Laura clapped her hands. 'Great thinking! Time that young devil paid us a visit!' The kettle began to whistle and she got up and made the tea, stirring it vigorously and pouring Nicola a large cup. 'Here, drink that down. You'll have to hurry if you're going to catch the nine o'clock bus back. I'll walk to the bus stop with you, Sheena and Herb could use some exercise.'

Nicola sat in the bus half an hour later and waved to Laura. As she watched the sturdy, bespectacled figure walk away, the two dogs following at her heels, she felt bleak and alone. When it really came down to it no one but she could make the decision and she was no nearer to it now than she had been last night. For what seemed hours she had lain awake in the darkness. Simon asking her to marry him was like a dream come true. Half of her longing to simply say yes, but at the back of her mind that small voice wouldn't be silenced. 'Does he love you? Can he ever love anyone else? Does he merely need a mother for Maria? Are you simply a convenient way out of a problem?' She thought of the way he had held her and kissed her—the tender passion that had made her heart sing with love for him—then she remembered Laura's words: 'What man wouldn't be flattered by the admiration of a young woman?' Maybe in the same circumstances any moderately attractive female would have evoked the same response. She pushed the thought from her with disgust. Laura was right of course. The best thing she could do would be to get involved in as many things as possible—starting with contacting Terry. She'd do it as soon as she got back to Meadowlands.

As she was walking up the drive she heard a voice calling her:

'Hey, Staff! Where's the fire?'

Looking round she saw Gerry Armstrong and stopped to wait while he caught her up. 'Hello, Gerry. What are you doing out here?'

'Taking a bit of a walk. I got fed up in there—no attractive company—no one willing to play Monopoly or Backgammon—not even anything on the telly.' He sighed. 'I wonder how long it'll be before I can get out of here and start *living* again!'

He looked restless and bored and Nicola took his arm sympathetically. 'It's no use trying to rush things, Gerry. I'm sure you know that. And it really isn't that bad in here, is it?'

He gave her his rueful, lop-sided grin. 'Of course

it isn't. I don't know what I'd have done without this place and all of you folks when things were bad. I didn't mean to sound ungrateful. It's just—'

'I know. It must be pretty frustrating for an active chap like you.' She smiled at him. 'Give me half an hour and I'll thrash you at Scrabble. How's that?'

He squeezed her arm. 'I thought you'd never ask! Just what I need to loosen my stiff fingers and your stiff brain!' He peered at her preoccupied face. 'Hey—what's up?'

She shook her head. 'Nothing—why?'

He shrugged. 'You're not reacting the way you usually do when I insult you. Got something on your mind?'

'Nothing that need bother you.'

He narrowed his eyes. 'Is that the way to talk to a mate? What with you and Natalie!'

'Oh, Natalie's back, is she?' she asked.

He nodded glumly. 'She didn't want to be bothered with me though. Straight up to her room, all starry-eyed. Something to do with that flash photographer guy she had a date with in London. Just my luck!'

'Well, it's nice that somebody's happy, isn't it?' Nicola said a trifle wistfully. 'And no one needs happiness more than Natalie.'

'What's he got that I haven't, I ask myself?' Gerry asked gloomily. 'You know, being in here gets you like that. My ego is in serious trouble and *that's* something I thought I'd never say!'

She laughed in spite of her mood. 'Poor Gerry. Look, I' going to ring my brother and ask him down here for a visit. Maybe he'll cheer you up. I have a feeling that he and you will get along. He makes musical instruments, you know.'

'Maybe he can smuggle me out of here inside a double bass or something!' He looked at her closely. 'Anyway—where have you been? It's not your day off, is it?'

'I've been to see my cousin.'

He laughed. 'Go on, pull the other one! You can tell me, Staff. I'm broad minded, even if I have been forced to live like a Trappist monk for the past few months. You slipped out to see a bloke, didn't you? Who was it then, same handsome doctor as before?'

'What do you mean—as before?' she asked brusquely.

'Ah, got you going now, haven't I?' he said cheekily. 'Don't you know, Staff, that when people haven't enough to think about they start taking a keen interest in other people's lives? Human nature, they call it. Come on—might as well satisfy my curiosity—who is it—Doc' Grey?'

'Oh Gerry, for heaven's sake be your age!' she snapped. 'What right have you to bombard me with personal questions? I may be on call practically twenty-four hours a day but I do have some right to privacy, surely!'

He stared at her, dismayed at her unexpectedly violent reaction to his teasing. 'All right, all right! Cool it, Staff. I was only egging you on for a bit of fun. Pardon me for living—can't seem to do anything right for anyone tonight!'

She looked at his crestfallen face and relented a little. 'I'm sorry, Gerry, I—'

'Don't give it another thought.' He walked away. 'And never mind the game. I'll take a raincheck.'

Nicola stared after him, biting her lip. He'd been so pleased to see her. She shouldn't have snapped at him like that—but he did go a bit far sometimes.

As she passed Natalie's room she hesitated, then lifted her hand and tapped softly. The girl's voice answered at once:

'Who is it?'

'It's only me, Staff.'

'Oh, come in.'

She found Natalie lying on her bed looking happier than she had seen her since she first came to Meadowlands. She smiled. 'I take it your day was a success.'

Natalie nodded. 'Wonderful. Rick was so good to me—took me out for a super lunch with some new friends and colleagues of his. He's going to develop the pictures he took and I'm going up again soon. He says he has an idea but he won't tell me anything about it yet—he says it's to be a surprise.' She sat up on the bed, hugging her knees. 'You know, Staff, when Rick looks at me in that special way of his I can almost believe I have no scars at all.'

'I told you so,' Nicola smiled. 'When you love someone things like that don't matter.'

During the week that followed she managed to avoid seeing Simon alone. He came to see Natalie between treatments at the hospital and she could feel his eyes on her, willing her to look at him. But as soon as the examination was over she made an excuse to Sister Martin and whisked away before he had a chance to speak. She received a letter from Terry, confirming that he was free and would be coming down to Hampshire the following week. Hearing his voice on the night she had telephoned him had cheered and comforted her.

'It'll be so lovely to see you again,' she told him. 'It seems like years.'

'What's all this about?' he sounded surprised. 'I didn't know you cared so much about your wandering minstrel brother.'

She laughed. Although she and Terry had always been close they had never been demonstrative towards each other. 'I'm longing to hear all your news, Terry. You're not the world's greatest letter writer!'

'Are you all right?' Terry had asked perceptively.

'Of course I am. I can look forward to seeing my brother without there being something wrong, can't I?'

'I don't know. You sound a bit choked. Maybe it's as well I'm coming down there to sort you out,' he told her.

'Cheek!' she muttered as she hung up. Terry was as bad as the rest of them—thinking of his presence as all-healing. How chauvinistic could he get?

She was remembering this conversation one morning as she came out of Sister's office where she had been to collect some notes. Head down, she hurried round a corner and cannoned straight into Simon.

'Oh! Sorry, I wasn't looking where I—' She tailed off as he took her by the shoulders and looked gravely into her eyes.

'Why have you been avoiding me?'

She felt her cheeks colouring. 'I—I haven't.'

He shook his head. 'We both know that you have. Look—Maria has been asking when you're coming to see her again. Can you come on your next day off? Tomorrow, isn't it?'

'I do have other demands on my free time, you know!' she said hotly.

His hands dropped to his sides. 'Of course you do. It was presumptuous of me to ask you.'

Immediately she was sorry. 'No, no, it's all right. Of course I'll come and see Maria. It was just—'

'Look, Nicola, can we talk?' He looked at his watch. 'When are you off duty?'

'Eight o'clock, but—'

'Come across to the Dower House—have supper with Maria and me.'

She racked her brain for an excuse, feeling trapped. 'I don't know—I—' At that moment one of the care assistants came round the corner and looked at them curiously. 'I really do have to go now,' Nicola said desperately.

'Eight o'clock then—you'll come?' His hand was on her arm.

She gave up. 'All right. I'll be there.' As she watched his tall figure walk away along the corridor she bit her lip. Tonight he would want his answer but what was she to say to him? If they were alone—if he kissed her again—she would be lost. How could she bear to tell him she had decided not to see him again when she loved him so?

She dressed carefully, choosing a skirt of rich burgundy corduroy and a matching angora sweater. This evening the air had the first chill of autumn to it. As she dressed she tried not to think about the coming evening or of what she would say. Nothing ever seemed to turn out the way she planned it anyway. Better to play it by ear, as Terry would say. She was just coming down the stairs when she almost bumped into Natalie. The girl's face was aglow with excitement.

'I've just had a call from Rick,' she told Nicola. 'I'm going up to London again tomorrow. I've just checked with Sister and she says it's all right. Rick says the shots he took of me have turned out fine and he may have a job lined up for me. Isn't it great? I can hardly believe it.'

'That's wonderful, Natalie. I told you everything would be all right, didn't I?' As she walked across the park Nicola wished that she were as good at putting her own life in order.

The dining room at the Dower House was delightful; furnished with dark oak furniture and a carpet of glowing red. In the fireplace a cheerful fire crackled, filling the room with the fragrance of apple logs. The long table was laid with care, silver and glass glinted in the firelight against the creamy lace of an antique table-cloth. Maria wore a pretty blue dress and her long hair was brushed back and tied with a matching ribbon. Nicola had the uncomfortable impression that it was a special occasion.

'It isn't anyone's birthday, is it?' she asked, sipping the sherry that Simon had poured for her.

Maria smiled. 'No, but we don't often have guests for dinner. Nanny and I thought it would be fun to make everything sort of special.' She looked anxiously from her father to Nicola. 'You do like it, don't you? I laid the table myself but the fire and Granny's table-cloth were Nanny's idea.'

Simon smiled. 'Of course we like it, darling. You've done everything beautifully.'

The meal was delicious and afterwards Mrs Dickens served coffee to them in the living room. Nicola noticed that as well as lighting a fire she had meticulously tidied the room; not a book was out of place, not a cushion rumpled. She was certainly an honoured guest. The thought made her uneasy.

When she came to take the coffee tray Mrs Dickens looked pointedly at Maria. 'Time you were thinking about bed, young lady.'

Maria looked up in dismay. 'Oh, Nanny, must I?' She looked appealingly at her father. 'Do I have to, Daddy?'

'I think you should do as Nanny says,' he told her. 'Perhaps Nicola will come and see you again tomorrow, if she isn't doing anything else, of course.' He gave Nicola a sidelong glance and she added:

'Yes, I'll come in the afternoon. Maybe we could go for a walk and take a packed tea with us.'

'Ooh—that would be fun!' Maria's face lit up and

Nicola felt a tug at her heart. It took so little to please the child. She felt guilty about her earlier remark to Simon.

After she had gone, hugging her father warmly and giving Nicola a soft kiss on the cheek, Simon looked at Nicola.

'You've made her very happy. Thank you.'

It wasn't fair. It was sheer blackmail and she wanted to tell him so. Instead she said: 'It's all right. She's a very sweet child and I enjoy her company.'

He moved across to sit beside her on the settee. 'And my company—do you enjoy that too, Nicola? It's almost a fortnight since I asked you to marry me. Have you given the matter any more thought?'

Had she given the matter any more thought! Nicola wanted to laugh at the sheer irony of it. There had scarcely been a waking moment when she hadn't thought about it! If only she were nearer to the answer. She avoided his eyes.

'I—can't marry you—at the moment, Simon,' she said haltingly.

There was a small silence. 'What do you mean by "at the moment"?' he asked gently.

She frowned. 'It's hard for me to explain why to you. Let's say that I just don't feel that the circumstances are right.'

'You don't feel we're compatible—is that it? In what way? Is it the age difference that worries you?'

She looked up at him in surprise. 'I can honestly say that I hadn't given that a thought,' she said truthfully.

'Then what?' There was an impatient edge to his voice now. 'Look, Nicola, we've known each other for a long time. In the Bishop's Wood days you had a—well a soft spot for me. It wasn't a secret, everyone knew about it. I—' He broke off as he noticed her scarlet cheeks.

'As you say that was a long time ago,' she said sharply. 'I wasn't aware that I was that obvious— some sort of hospital joke!'

He winced. 'Nicola, it wasn't like that at all. I put it clumsily.' He took her hand in both of his. 'You were very young—naive. You hadn't learned to disguise your feelings or the way you looked at me. Believe me, I found it very flattering and very sweet.'

She pulled her hand away. 'And you thought I'd been nursing that same schoolgirl crush all this time?'

'Nicola, darling, please don't let's play games with each other. Surely we can be honest. We're both adults now. You're not going to pretend that your response to me the other night was anything but genuine?'

She started to protest but before she could say anything he took her face in his hands and stopped her with a kiss. At first she held herself stiff and unresponsive, but his lips finally claimed hers with tender persistence, teasing them with soft persuasion till they surrendered to him. She melted against him, her arms creeping round his neck as he gathered her close. Together they sank back against the cushions and all her senses fused into a surge of longing. Urgent warning signals sounded in the back of her mind but she ignored them, driven only by the powerful urge within her. As their lips parted she laid her head against his shoulder, breathing his name against the warm skin of his throat. 'Simon—oh, Simon.'

He brushed his cheek against her hair. 'I could make you happy, Nicola,' he whispered. 'And I know you could make us happy.'

She jerked her head up. 'Us?' she questioned.

A small frown darkened his eyes. 'Maria and I. Darling, we must be realistic. The woman I marry must make Maria happy too—but that isn't a problem. It's marvellous that you and she get along so well together.'

She moved away from him, swallowing hard. 'Simon—you know you only have to ask me if you want someone to help Maria. You don't need to make a lifelong sacrifice!'

He stared at her angrily. 'What kind of remark is that? Lifelong sacrifice!'

She stood up and walked away towards the fireplace—as far from his disturbing closeness as she could. By the time she turned to face him again she had controlled her features if not her emotions.

'You said just now that we should be honest with each other, Simon,' she said. 'It's true that I was in—that I had a crush on you four years ago, but I've grown up a lot since then. You need a wife—a mother figure for Maria and a—a—loving companion for yourself. But I have certain ideals. I want to come first in the heart of the man I marry and I know I can never do that with you.'

He shook his head, frowning. 'I don't know what you're talking about!'

'I think you do,' she went on, getting into her stride now, relieved to be letting out all the doubts and misgivings that had been gnawing at her for the past two weeks. 'You thought no doubt that I'd be ideal for you. I get along well with your daughter; I'm a nurse, so I'd understand your work and not make undue demands on your time and attention and, above all, you remembered the crush I had on you four years ago—the laughs it gave you when you caught me looking at you like a—like a—*sick sheep*. It must have given you enormous satisfaction when I fell so neatly into your arms—' Her voice caught huskily in her throat. 'Instant success, you might call it. A labour-saving courtship—dinner-date to register office in one easy step. And I'm not beautiful so you wouldn't have to worry too much about competition—'

'*Stop it!* How dare you say that to me?' He sprang to his feet, his face white with anger and strode across the room towards her. Taking her by the shoulders he shook her roughly. 'I believe you're hysterical, Nicola, though heaven knows why. What you're saying is sheer nonsense.'

'It isn't—no, it *isn't*.' She stared up at him with tear-filled eyes. 'There'll never be another woman for you, Simon and we both know it. At Bishop's Wood your marriage was the envy of everyone who knew you. I'm sorry if it went wrong and I don't want to cause you any more pain but I can see—'

She broke off seeing from the expression on his face that she had gone too far—that she was almost out of her depth. Simon gripped her shoulders painfully, pressing her backwards in an attempt to make her look at him.

'Go on—what can you see?' His voice was ominously quiet. 'You may as well finish now that you've started. I'm finding all this very educational!'

She shook her head, tears beginning to trickle down her cheeks. 'I can see that—when you look at me—when you're kissing me—you're really wishing it's Claudia you're holding in your arms,' she whispered. 'And it will never—*never* be any different.'

For a long moment he stood staring down at her as though stunned, till, unable to bear the tension any longer she wrenched herself from his grasp and fled from the room—out of the house, crossing the park at a stumbling run, anxious only to put as much distance between Simon and herself as she could.

She didn't stop running until she reached the rear door that led to her flat. Fumbling in her bag for the key she let herself in and leant against the door, the breath rasping in her throat. Well, that was that—she'd said it—all of it. All the doubts and resentments, the fears and dreads had come tumbling out. Now Simon knew exactly how she felt—and he hadn't denied a single word of it. Obviously all her suspicions were well founded. Wearily she dragged herself upstairs and closed the door of her room.

With the door locked and the curtains drawn, in a small private world of her own she could give way to the great tide of tears she had been holding back. She threw herself down on the bed and gave herself up to it.

CHAPTER EIGHT

'You know, I think you'll be able to come into Medchester for your physio next week, Gerry—under your own steam, I mean.' Geoff Carter, the visiting physio stood back to smile at Nicola. 'He's done really well, hasn't he, Staff?'

Nicola nodded. 'He has, the only problem now is stopping him from trying to run before he can walk—literally in this case!'

'You've got to be joking,' Gerry said wryly, climbing down from the massage plinth where Geoff had been working on his legs. 'Let's face it, I'll never do a four-minute mile now. Still, there are compensations.' He patted his legs as he tied the belt of his bathrobe. 'Enough steel plates in these two babies to build a battle ship. Any girl fancies me, all she has to do is hide a magnet in her handbag and I won't even be able to run away!' He assumed an expression of bliss. 'What a way to go, eh, Geoff?'

Geoff looked at Nicola and they both laughed as Gerry went off to have his shower. 'He's a great guy, isn't he?' Geoff said.

Nicola nodded. 'He is. I must admit that I've got a very soft spot for him. He's been through terrible pain since his accident, yet he's always cheerful.'

'Does he have many visitors?' Geoff asked.

'No, oddly enough. He has no family of course and I have an idea he's told his racing friends not to come until he gives them permission. Gerry wouldn't want anyone feeling sorry for him.'

'Did he ever tell you that his girl ditched him?' Geoff asked her.

She shook her head. 'No—no, he didn't. Poor Gerry.' She lapsed into thoughtful silence as Geoff took off his white coat. He glanced at her.

'I thought Thursday was your day off. Have you changed with someone else this week?'

'No, one of the care assistants is off sick so I volunteered to help out this morning.' In actual fact she had been glad to. The idea of her own company was anathema.

'I see. When are you off?' Geoff asked.

'Any moment now. I'll be free as soon as the next shift comes on.'

Something in her tone made him look sharply at her. 'If you're going into Medchester I can give you a lift if you like. I can hang on for you if you want to change. I'm not in a hurry.'

But she shook her head. 'I have to go somewhere this afternoon—here in Farthingbridge, I mean.'

'Well, we could have a bite of lunch if you feel like it. It's a lovely day. Maybe we could find one of those thatched pubs the Forest is so famous for.'

She looked up at him and saw that his hazel eyes held concern for her. 'That's very kind of you, Geoff. I'd like that very much.'

He ran a hand through his unruly auburn hair. 'Not at all. You're not the kind of girl one expects to find at a loose end. Call it my good luck!'

They found a little pub that had tables outside and ate ploughman's lunches in the sunshine. Geoff asked how she was settling down and she shrugged non-committally.

'It's a great contrast to city life, but I like it—and the work, of course.'

'How do you manage for social life?' he asked. 'Farthingbridge isn't exactly what you could call swinging, is it?'

She had an idea he was fishing and she decided to change the subject. 'I've been thinking of getting myself a little car so that I can take myself out and about more,' she told him. 'But I don't really know how to go about it.'

He rose to the bait. 'I can help you there. Do you drive?'

She nodded. 'I did pass my test some time ago, but I haven't driven much since. I think I'd need a refresher course.'

He grinned at her enthusiastically. 'Great. May I offer my services? I taught my sister to drive and she passed her test first time. Tell you what—until you get your own car you could have some lessons in mine. My insurance will cover you.'

She bit her lip. She had dropped neatly into this and now she couldn't think of any way to get out of it. She made a sudden decision. Why shouldn't she accept Geoff's offer? He was young—about her own age—they had much in common and she liked him. She smiled into his freckled face.

'Thank you, Geoff. That would be marvellous.'

'Great! I can come over and pick you up in the evenings,' he said eagerly. 'We'd better not waste any time either. Before you know it the nights will be closing in and the winter will be here. I'll keep an eye open for a car for you too. A cousin of mine has a garage. What sort were you thinking of?'

'I don't know—a Mini or something,' she told him. 'Something that will be easy to manage and economical to run.'

He nodded. 'Fine. I'll look out for one.' There was a silence as they finished their food, then Geoff asked: 'Where are you going this afternoon—if you don't mind me asking, that is?'

She smiled. 'I'm taking Maria Grey for a picnic— you know, Simon Grey's daughter.'

He looked impressed. 'Wow! Elevated company you keep, don't you?'

She coloured slightly. 'I knew the family when I was doing my training at Bishop's Wood four years ago,' she explained.

'I see.' He looked thoughtful. 'He's a brilliant surgeon, but I imagine he's not too easy to get to know.'

'Why do you say that?'

He pulled a face. 'He seems sort of withdrawn. Pleasant enough but—*removed*—as though there's a barrier between him and other people. Of course the talk is that he never got over the death of his wife.' He looked at her. 'You must have known her too. What was she like? Was she as beautiful as everyone says?'

Nicola's heart felt as though it were being

squeezed in a vice. 'Yes,' she said quietly. 'I think she was the most beautiful woman I've ever seen.'

He sighed. 'Poor bloke. It's sad, isn't it?'

Nicola nodded slowly. 'Yes,' she said. 'Yes—it's sad.'

As she walked across the park that afternoon she thought about Natalie. She had gone off to London that morning in a state of high excitement. Things really seemed to be working out for her and Nicola felt a warm glow of satisfaction when she remembered that it had been she who had put her on the right path. Since Rick Milton had come back into her life she had looked a different girl; her eyes glowed, she took more interest in her appearance and her general outlook on life had improved dramatically. Nicola reflected that it was a little frightening that one human being—one *man*—could have that much influence, but while things were going so well for Natalie who was she to question the reason?

Maria was waiting at the gate of the Dower House, dressed in jeans and a T-shirt. When she saw Nicola coming she waved excitedly and ran to meet her.

'As it's such a warm day I thought we might go to Pixie Lake,' she said eagerly. 'It's quite a long way but Nanny says you can borrow her bike if you like—and she's packed us a super tea.'

Nicola held up the bag she was carrying. 'But I didn't mean her to do that! It was my suggestion and I've brought the tea.'

Maria waved a hand airily. 'Oh, don't worry about that. Nanny loves messing about with sandwiches and things. She's made us some of her special little cakes too.'

Nicola looked up as the housekeeper came out to join them. She was carrying a wicker picnic basket which she strapped onto the carrier of a bicycle leaning against the wall. Nicola shook her head.

'You really shouldn't have gone to all this trouble. I meant to bring the tea myself.' She held up the bag. 'I have, in fact.'

Maud Dickens smiled at her. 'Never mind, Miss Page. We'll put your tea in the freezer and then I can put my feet up another day.'

Nicola turned to Maria. 'Where is this Pixie Lake? I don't think I've ever heard of it.'

'That's only Maria's name for it,' Mrs Dickens told her. 'It's about three miles from here. A lake formed by the site of an old gravel pit that was worked out years ago. They say that the minerals in the soil give the water its curious brilliant blue colour.' She gave a slight shudder. 'It's pretty enough but I think it's an eerie place.'

'An *enchanted* place,' Maria corrected. 'They say it's fathomless and that if you make a wish on a special day in the year, your wish will come true.'

Nicola laughed. 'And is this the "special day"?'

Maria shook her head. 'No one knows for sure what day it is. I always make a wish every time I go—just in case. One day it's sure to be the right day.'

Nicola carefully mounted the bicycle. 'Well, all I

wish at this moment is that I haven't forgotten how to ride a bike!' she laughed.

After the first few wobbly minutes she got the hang of it and began to enjoy her ride, Maria pacing her, her long legs pushing energetically on the pedals.

The lake lived up to Maria's description, lying smooth and incredibly blue under a clear sky. Around three sides of it steep slopes were covered in lush green vegetation while on the fourth side a strip of gleaming white sand formed a tiny 'beach'. They leaned the bikes against a tree and Nicola spread the rug they had brought with them. Maria threw herself full length on it and rolled onto her back to gaze up at the sky.

'Isn't this a lovely place?'

Nicola stood looking round her. The place had a strange beauty but Mrs Dickens had been right, there was an odd feel about it—an unnaturalness that made her shiver. 'It's very quiet,' she said.

Maria sat up and hugged her knees. 'That's what I like about it. I always feel when I come here that if I listen very carefully I might hear something that no one has ever heard before.'

Nicola looked at her. 'What do you mean—what sort of thing?'

The child shrugged. 'I don't know—something magic—the cry of a swan maybe. I've never met anyone who's heard that. They only do it once you know, just before they die.'

Nicola joined her on the rug. 'You're a funny girl. Why would you like to hear that?'

Maria frowned, drawing her smooth childish brow into furrows of concentration.

'It's hard to explain. I just feel that if I heard it it might make me know—other things—secrets.'

'Any particular secret?' Nicola asked.

Maria's little pointed face was grave. 'That's something else I don't know. I think there is something special but I can't remember what. Sometimes when I first wake up in the mornings it's almost there—but then it goes away, like a dream.'

Her dark eyes were troubled and Nicola got up and began to open the picnic hamper. 'Perhaps some food will help,' she said cheerfully. 'Give me a hand to unpack it, will you?'

Mrs Dickens had packed enough food to feed an army. There were sandwiches with various fillings, homemade cakes and chocolate biscuits, cheese, fruit and a huge flask of iced lemonade. As they ate Nicola looked at the little girl opposite her. One day she would be as beautiful as her mother, but at the moment she was like a young foal, all long limbs and flying mane. She thought about the strange things the child had said. Obviously she was too solitary—too much alone. Could it be that the memory of the accident still lurked at the back of her mind, half blocked by the trauma? Would it be a good thing if she were to remember the full horror of that night or not?

'Tell me more about yourself, Maria,' she invited. 'About school and your friends there. It'll soon be time to go back, won't it? What do you want to do when you grow up?'

Maria sighed and fixed her eyes on the far side of the lake. 'School is all right, I suppose. I like English and history best. I haven't really got any friends. I don't think people like me very much.' Thoughtfully she scooped up a handful of the fine sand and let it trickle through her fingers. 'When I grow up I *think* I'd like to be a doctor, like Daddy.' She looked up at Nicola suddenly. 'My mummy was an artist. Did you know that? I like art, but I'm not very good at it.'

After a moment Nicola said: 'You must miss your mother.'

The child shook her head, oddly detached. 'Not really. You see I don't remember her. I only know what people tell me.' She smiled. 'I remembered you though, didn't I? That's funny really because—' She stopped talking suddenly to stare across the lake. 'Look!' She pointed.

Nicola followed her gaze and saw a family of swans sailing majestically across the water; cob and pen and six cygnets, their brown feathers almost completely replaced by white. She smiled, shading her eyes to see them more clearly. 'Aren't they lovely?' she said. 'They must have a nest over there somewhere. Shall we see if they'll feed from us? There are still a couple of sandwiches left.'

'No!' Maria scrambled to her feet and backed away, her eyes wide with fear. 'Please, Nicola— let's go. Let's go now!'

'Why? They won't hurt us. It's a pity to go so soon.' But Maria was throwing things into the basket in a panic.

'I don't want to hear them cry—I don't want them to die. I don't *care* about the secret. I don't want to know what it is!'

With a shock Nicola saw the terror in the child's eyes and got up at once to help pack the things away. She couldn't pretend to understand why Maria should be so disturbed. All she knew was that the sooner they left this place, the better.

They cycled in silence for a while. Nicola felt instinctively that Maria must have time to recover —that she must be the one to break the silence. When at last she did it was as though the incident at the lakeside had never happened.

'There'll soon be blackberries,' she said brightly. 'Daddy and I usually get lots. It's fun. Maybe this year you can come with us.'

Nicola was reminded of her own problems and her heart sank. She wondered uneasily whether Simon would be at the Dower House when they got back and how she would face him if he was. 'We'll see,' she said abstractedly.

'Do you like blackberries?' Maria asked conversationally. 'We do. Nanny makes pies and jam with them—wine too, but I'm not allowed to have any of that.'

As they cycled along the forest track the clear skies began to cloud over and a chill wind sprang up. Nicola reflected that they hadn't been a moment too soon in leaving the lake. They would be lucky to get back to the Dower House before the storm broke. The first drops of rain began to fall as they were putting their bikes away in the garage and they ran to the back door, carrying the picnic basket between them. Mrs Dickens was in the hall, speaking to someone on the telephone and Nicola began to unpack the basket and wash up the plates and beakers. She turned as the door opened and the housekeeper came into the kitchen.

'Oh, thank goodness you're back!'

'Yes. We were lucky to beat the storm—' She stopped as she saw the expression on the woman's face. 'What is it—is anything wrong?'

'You're wanted at Meadowlands at once,' Mrs Dickens told her. 'That was Sister Martin on the phone. I'm to ring round and see if I can locate Mr Grey. You can take my bike if you like. It'll be quicker for you.' She turned to go back to the telephone.

'But what's happened?' Nicola called after her. 'Did Sister say?'

'I don't know any details, just that it's Miss Fryer. She's been taken poorly.'

Nicola dried her hands and looked at Maria. 'You'll finish these things for Nanny, won't you? Sorry I have to dash off like this.'

'Will you come again soon?' The huge brown eyes looked up appealingly at her.

Impulsively Nicola dropped a kiss on the child's head. 'Of course I will.'

The rain was falling heavily as she pedalled across the park on the borrowed bike. What could have happened to Natalie, she wondered? Deep inside her an uneasiness stirred. Could it have anything to do with Rick Milton?

Sister Martin met her at the foot of the stairs. 'Sorry to have to fetch you back like this on your day off, Staff. Perhaps you've heard. It's Natalie.'

Nicola ran her fingers through her dripping hair. 'What's wrong with her?'

Sister lowered her voice. 'Heaven knows what happened in London today. She must have come back early, though I didn't know she was in the building. Luckily Gerry Armstrong found her. She was in a terrible state—It seems she'd bought a bottle of aspirin tablets on her way home and—' She looked at Nicola, her face grim. 'Need I go on?'

Nicola gasped. 'Oh God! Is she all right?'

'Fortunately yes. She hadn't had time to take all that many when Gerry found her. I must say he acted with great presence of mind. By the time I arrived on the scene he'd administered the only first aid he knew and persuaded her to part with them. I've given her an emetic too but I'm afraid she's still badly shocked, poor child.' She turned to lead the way upstairs, continuing as she went, 'I've sent for Mr Grey. He understands her. I don't feel it would be wise to send her into hospital under the circumstances. I believe she'll recover better here where she has friends around her, but I want him to confirm my decision.'

Nicola's heart was heavy as she turned over the possible causes of Natalie's distress. 'Has she said why she did it?' she asked.

Sister shook her head. 'No—time enough to ask her about that later. But I thought that if she wanted to talk you would be the one she'd want.

That's why I sent for you.' They stopped outside Natalie's door and Sister smiled at her. 'Go in and sit with her awhile. She needs sleep, but if there's anything she wants to get off her chest it might help her.'

Inside the room Nicola closed the door softly behind her. The girl lay with her face to the wall. She pulled a chair up to the bed and gently touched Natalie's shoulder.

'Natalie—it's me—Staff. I'm sorry, is there anything I can do?'

The face that turned to look at her was puffy with weeping, the eyes red-rimmed. 'I think you've done enough!' She hissed the words at Nicola, looking at her with something like hate in her anguished eyes. 'Why couldn't you mind your own business? Why didn't you leave me alone? If Rick hadn't seen me like this he would never have got the idea!' Her voice was almost incoherent with sobs as she buried her face in the pillow. 'Oh God—why didn't you let me die?'

Nicola reached out to touch her heaving shoulder. 'Please, Natalie, don't cry like that—let me help you—' She turned as she heard the door open behind her and her heart contracted as she saw Simon standing there. She stood up but he barely glanced at her as he said coldly:

'I think you'd better leave her to me.'

She went silently from the room.

It seemed hours before he came down the stairs. Nicola was waiting at the bottom. Her eyes searched his face as he came towards her but she could read nothing in his expression.

'Come into Sister's office, please,' he said. 'I want to speak to you.'

With a heavy heart she followed him into Sister's office. He closed the door quietly and turned to look at her.

'I understand it was you who contacted this Milton man,' he said. 'How could you have acted so irresponsibly? Surely your basic training as a nurse taught you never to involve yourself in the patients' personal lives!'

She bit her lip. 'Natalie was becoming so withdrawn. She had an exaggerated impression of the severity of her scarring. She'd confided in me about Rick Milton—she told me they were close but that there'd been a misunderstanding. It was obvious that she was eating her heart out for him and I thought—'

'It wasn't up to you to make judgments.' His voice cut through her words. 'If it hadn't been for Gerry Armstrong finding her as he did you might have had something much worse than this on your conscience!'

'I don't even know what happened,' Nicola said unhappily. 'She wouldn't talk to me.'

'Then I'll tell you!' Simon put his hand in his inside pocket and took out an envelope. He opened it and threw the contents across Sister's desk towards her. 'These are the direct result of your interference,' he told her coldly. 'And thanks to them Natalie has taken a damaging regressive step in her recovery.'

Nicola was staring at the photographs that lay face upwards on the desk. They were of Natalie—some taken in a bad light showed her scars at their worst while others had been retouched so that the scars were barely visible. She looked up at him frowning.

'What were they intended for?' she asked.

His eyes were like flint as he looked at her. 'They were intended as an advertising inducement for a cosmetic surgery clinic newly opened in London. A "before and after" if you like.'

Nicola's eyes widened. 'But—surely that's illegal?'

'Illegal, yes, but brutally cruel to Natalie, wouldn't you say?'

'And it's all my fault.' Nicola swallowed hard. 'I'll see to it that you have my resignation in the morning,' she whispered.

'Oh no! You don't get away with it as easily as that!' he told her. 'You must surely agree that the least you can do is to stay here and see that you put matters right.' His voice was harsh. 'I always said that it was a mistake, stepping into a branch of nursing you knew so little about. Now you've proved me right, unfortunately. All you can hope to do is to make it up to Natalie in any way you can. But please remember in future, Staff Nurse Page, your job is to nurse and to give your support and encouragement to the patients, *not* to involve yourself in their personal affairs.'

'I see—' Her heart was beating uncomfortably fast. He was taking his anger with her into their work. It was unfair and she wanted to tell him so. 'It must be very gratifying always being *right* in everything you do,' she said bitterly. 'I regret what has happened very much but it was done with the best of motives. We can't all be perfect!'

He stared at her for a long moment. 'I am speaking to you professionally. Please don't make matters any more difficult than they already are,' he said quietly. He picked up the photographs and slipped them back into the envelope. 'I shall take these away with me,' he said. 'The fewer people who see them, the better. If it were not for Natalie I would take action against Milton. As it is I shall have to satisfy myself with a warning letter to him. He should consider himself extremely lucky.'

Nicola took a step towards him, her throat constricting with tears. How could she stay here now? It would be impossible for her. 'Please—I want to leave Meadowlands. It isn't only because of Natalie and what has happened. I—don't have to make myself any clearer, do I?'

He walked to the door and then turned to look at her. 'I can assure you that you have nothing to fear from me,' he said coldly. 'You have made it abundantly clear that you feel we have nothing to offer each other as two human beings. In future if I wish to communicate with you I will do it through Sister Martin.' And, turning on his heel he left the office, closing the door firmly.

CHAPTER NINE

NICOLA had never been more glad of a weekend off and when she arrived at Laura's cottage late on Friday evening the older woman was quite shocked by her appearance.

'Good heavens, child! What on earth has happened to make you look like this? You look as though you haven't slept for a week!'

'Only one night, to be precise.' Nicola flopped into a chair. 'Oh, Laura—if only I didn't have to go back there ever again!' All the way to Milton Green on the bus she had been promising herself that she wouldn't tell Laura about what had happened—wouldn't let her see how miserable she was. But somehow, the moment she was inside the dear familar four walls and in Laura's comforting presence all her resolve left her and the tears began to flow.

Laura sat down in the chair opposite, her eyes concerned as she looked at Nicola's crumpled face and shaking shoulders. She had never seen the girl so unhappy and all her maternal instincts were aroused. Obviously it was that man again! But she knew better than to condemn him too vehemently.

'Tell me about it, Nicky,' she invited gently. 'Come on, love, better get it all off your chest.'

Nicola poured it all out to her cousin, starting with the day she had decided to telephone Rick Milton on Natalie's behalf and ending with the row she had had with Simon yesterday. When she had finished Laura shook her head.

'Well, I'm sorry to have to say it, dear, but he was right. You know, what you did really was asking for trouble. It might have been excusable if you had known the man personally, but you didn't, did you? He could have been the worst kind of unscrupulous villain—as indeed he was!'

Nicola nodded. 'I know. I was wrong and I admit it. I could even put up with the way people keep looking at me, but Simon—and the way he spoke—after—after—' she couldn't go on for the fresh flood of tears that began and Laura moved across to comfort her.

'Oh dear,' she sighed. 'It's a pity you had to go and get emotionally involved. I'm beginning to think you were right in the first place, when you said it would be a mistake to work with him. Have you thought of leaving?'

Nicola looked up at her. 'He won't let me. He says I have to stay on and put right the damage I've done.'

'That's nonsense. He can't stop you if you really want—' Laura's eyes narrowed and she was about to add something, then thought better of it, contenting herself with patting Nicola's shoulder. 'All right then. If you're committed to staying on show him what you're made of. Prove just how good a nurse you really are. One thing about this kind of set-back, love. It teaches you a lesson you never forget.'

'But when I think what almost happened—*would* have happened if it hadn't been for Gerry Armstrong,' Nicola wailed. 'Sister Martin must feel I've let her down terribly and Natalie still won't speak to me.'

'You'll live it down,' Laura said briskly. 'I always say that no matter how bad things look at the time something good always comes out of it in the end. Try to relax and let things take their course. Make up your mind to enjoy life more in the future. You've wasted too much time crying for the moon!'

Nicola knew what her cousin was trying to say, even though she didn't put it into words. She really would have to try to have more social life, but she couldn't have had less enthusiasm for it. However, the following morning fate seemed to take matters out of her hands.

The telephone rang as they were having breakfast. Laura answered it and came back into the dining room with a smile on her face.

'It's for you. A young man who calls himself Geoff Carter. Ring a bell?'

Nicola drank the last of her coffee and got up from the table. 'He's the visiting physio.' She went into the hall and picked up the receiver. 'Hello. Nicola Page here.'

'Nicola—it's me—Geoff Carter. Look, I think I've found just the car for you. I rang Meadowlands and they gave me this number. If you're off this weekend perhaps you'd be free to look at this car with me. Or do you have anything else planned?'

Nicola felt her spirits rise. 'No, I'm free. What's it like, this car you've found?'

'Great—and I mean it,' he told her enthusiastically. 'It belongs to a rather eccentric old lady who's hardly used it. Apparently she's always treated it as though it were some kind of pet. It's in immaculate condition. I'm told that if it happened to rain she took a taxi instead! She's only selling because her eyesight is failing.'

'How about the price?' Nicola asked suspiciously. 'If it's that good—'

'The price is very low because of the year. She's had it quite a long time. But my cousin has looked it over and he assures me it's fine. He would have taken it in for her but—and listen to this. This is the best bit—' Nicola could hear the amusement in his voice. 'She wants to sell it herself because she says she'll only let it go to a "good home". She wants to see the person who buys it for herself. How about it then? If you're free I could take you along to see her this morning.'

Nicola laughed. 'I'd love to go—even if it's only to see an old lady who wants a good home for her car!'

'Tell me how to find you and I'll be there in about an hour,' he said.

Nicola was still smiling when she rejoined Laura at the breakfast table.

'Well, that's a better face than I've seen for some time!' Laura remarked. 'What did he want?' Nicola told her and she beamed. 'Well, maybe your luck is turning after all. The car sounds just what you've been looking for. How nice of this young man to go to so much trouble on your behalf.' She peered at Nicola. 'Nice, is he?'

'Very, but don't start getting any ideas,' Nicola told her firmly. 'Romance has no place in my life at the moment and I intend to keep it that way!'

'Mmm—' Laura got up and began to clear the table. 'I only wish I could believe it!' she muttered under her breath.

Geoff was as good as his word and arrived on the stroke of ten o'clock. Laura obviously took to him on sight and stood at the gate waving them off cheerfully. Nicola fell in love with the little car the moment she saw it. Sprayed a jaunty pillar-box red with beige upholstery, it gleamed in the sunlight as though it had just driven off the assembly line. Mrs Jimson, its owner looked at it fondly.

'I shall miss her so much,' she said sadly. 'She's been such a good friend to me. I wouldn't dream of letting her go if it wasn't for my eyes not being what they were, you know.' She looked Nicola up and down approvingly. 'But I can see that you'll take good care of her just as I have. She's only ever had the best oil and petrol and I never, *never* let her stand out in the rain.' She frowned anxiously. 'Let me see, you did say you had a nice garage for her, didn't you dear?'

'The use of one, yes,' Nicola assured her.

'Miss Page is a Staff Nurse at Meadowlands Rehabilitation Centre,' Geoff told the old lady with a twinkle in his eye. 'She's very good at taking care of people.'

Old Mrs Jimson fixed him with a beady eye. 'Are you making fun of me, young man?' she asked sternly.

Geoff coloured to the roots of his red hair. 'Me? Good heavens, no, Mrs Jimson! I feel the same about my own car.'

Nicola hoped that Mrs Jimson hadn't caught sight of Geoff's car. It was far from new or smart and it didn't look in the least cherished. 'May we talk about a price?' she asked hurriedly.

Half an hour later as they drove away she felt slightly dazed. She was the owner of a car for the first time in her life. Geoff had promised to take her round to his insurance agent, who, he said, would be able to give Nicola a cover note so that she could collect her car that afternoon.

'I don't know if I dare drive,' she said. 'It's about a year since I last did. I'm really very inexperienced.'

Geoff grinned at her. 'That means I shall have to devote my weekend to helping you get the hang of it all over again,' he told her cheerfully.

'Oh—but I wouldn't dream of taking up your time,' Nicola protested, but he laughed.

'Just let anyone try and stop me!'

After they had visited the insurance agent Geoff suggested lunch. Nicola rang Laura.

'You'd better expect me when you see me,' she said. 'I've bought this car and Geoff is going with me to collect it this afternoon.'

'Marvellous. I'm so glad. Don't hurry home, just concentrate on enjoying yourself,' Laura said happily.

They ate a hurried snack lunch, then Geoff parked his car in a long-stay car park quite close to where Mrs Jimson lived. As she drove the little car away Nicola was acutely aware of the little figure standing at the gate, waving a lace-edged handkerchief. She imagined that once they were out of sight the poor little old lady might have another use for it and she voiced this thought to Geoff. He laughed.

'You're as bad as she is! Just concentrate on your driving. You're doing fine.'

After a mile or two she lost her nervousness and began to enjoy herself. Now that she had her own car life would certainly be a lot easier, especially with the winter coming on. It really had been a good idea of Laura's. Suddenly she came out of her reverie, aware that Geoff was speaking to her.

'So you've really settled at Meadowlands, then?'

All at once the mention of the place brought back the events of the previous week, bringing her down to earth with a bump. The little car swerved as she took her eyes off the road.

'Hey, watch it!' Geoff warned.

Nicola drew into the side of the road and switched off the engine. He looked at her.

'Sorry. I didn't mean to put you off. Is anything the matter?'

She sighed. 'Yes—everything as a matter of fact. I've had a particularly trying week and your mentioning Meadowlands reminded me of it.'

'Oh dear—want to talk about it?' he asked.

She lifted her shoulders. 'It wouldn't help. Anyway, other people's troubles always sound trivial and boring. I'm trying to forget it, or at least to live it down.'

He looked puzzled. 'It sounds bad.'

'I made a pretty terrible mistake,' she confessed. 'It could have been critical but I was lucky. I shan't make the same mistake again.'

'Well, it looks as though we shall have to do our best to make you forget, doesn't it? What'll it be—a film, or—I know, the local Rep'! I believe the Medchester Players are doing a new comedy this week. Just the thing to cheer you up. Shall we drive over and see if they have any seats left?'

Nicola smiled. He really was nice. 'Why not? I could do with something to make me laugh.'

They managed to get the last two stalls at Medchester's Theatre Royal. There was an hour and a half to wait before the performance and Geoff suggested dinner in the theatre's Green Room. He was good company and Nicola soon found herself smiling again. The local company was very good and the play was well written and brilliantly funny. By the time the curtain fell on the second act Nicola had laughed a lot and felt relaxed. Geoff turned to her.

'This is the long interval. Do you fancy a drink?'

She smiled. 'I'd love one.'

They struggled through the press of people to the bar and Geoff found two seats. 'You sit tight while I get the drinks,' he told her. 'I'll be as quick as I can.'

She sat down to wait for him, looking round at the other members of the audience, then suddenly she froze in her seat. Not six feet away stood a tall familiar figure, his back towards her. He was with an attractive elegantly dressed woman of about thirty who was looking intently up into his eyes, taking in every word he said. In a panic Nicola looked around for another seat but the place was packed. Anyway, if she moved Geoff wouldn't know where to find her. She sat there in an agony of suspense, willing Simon not to turn round and see her.

'Phew! What a crush.' Geoff sank gratefully into the opposite seat then looked uncertainly at her. 'What's the matter? You did say sherry, didn't you?'

'What? Oh, yes—lovely!' Nicola picked up her glass and downed the drink at one gulp while Geoff looked on in amusement.

'Well, you obviously needed that! Shall I try and get you another?'

She coloured. 'Oh no. It's just that the time is getting on. Shall we get back to our seats now?'

He laughed. 'Give me a chance to finish my drink first. I fought hard enough to get it!' He picked up his glass and drank in what seemed to Nicola a maddeningly slow way. She prayed that Simon and his companion would move away before he noticed them, but she was out of luck. Just as Geoff was about to put down his empty glass Simon turned, looking for somewhere to deposit his own glass.

Their eyes met and held for a moment. She gave him a tremulous smile.

'Good evening.'

He nodded, glancing at Geoff, then, taking his companion by the arm he led her across the crowded room. Nicola let out her breath slowly as Geoff watched her.

'Didn't expect to see him out on the town,' he remarked.

'Who was that with him?' Nicola asked, unable to contain her curiosity.

'Helen Frazer. She's Mr Murdoch's new registrar,' he told her. 'You know, the ENT man at Medchester General.' He grinned. 'Quite a dish, isn't she? Grey's a dark horse—must be recovering from his depression at last as well he might with a girl like that to help him!' He looked at her and the smile left his face. 'What is it, Nicola? Aren't you feeling well?'

She pulled herself together. 'I'm fine thanks. It's a bit hot in here, that's all.'

She didn't take in one word of the third act. All she could think about was Simon—was he enjoying himself with the young woman doctor? Would she be able to get out of the theatre without seeing them again?

Almost before she knew it the curtain was coming down. The audience applauded; calls were taken, then the lights were going up and Geoff was helping her into her coat.

'I'll have to drop you off at the car park where you left your car,' she reminded him.

'How about you—will you be all right driving back to Milton Green on your own in the dark?' he asked her.

'I'll be fine, honestly. I have to start sometime.' As she spoke her eyes raked the auditorium but she couldn't see Simon anywhere. She heaved a sigh of relief.

In the theatre car park she looked up at him as she unlocked the door of the Mini. 'Geoff. I want to thank you for everything you've done for me to-day,' she said. 'It's been a super day—getting the car and everything—just what I needed to cheer me up. I don't know how to thank you.'

He smiled down at her. 'I can think of a very simple and effective way.' His hands cupped her face. 'It's this.' As he kissed her the headlights of a car swung across the car park, illuminating them in their bright light. Nicola froze but Geoff held her fast.

'Never mind them,' he whispered. 'They don't *have* to look and if they do they'll only envy me.' He kissed her again but as he moved away she was in time to see the number plate of the car that had passed. It was Simon's dark blue saloon. She groaned inwardly. Surely after tonight there could be no hope of mending their tattered relationship.

CHAPTER TEN

By the time Nicola reported for duty on Monday morning she was feeling much stronger. Her weekend had done her good in spite of the embarrassment of seeing Simon at the theatre. She had made up her mind to overcome her mistake and somehow make it up to Natalie. There had to be a way and she would find it. She was just coming out of the dining room after breakfast when Sister Martin caught her.

'Ah, Staff. Gerry Armstrong is going into Medchester this morning for his check up and final X-rays. I'd like you to go with him. As you'll be on official duty you can stay in your uniform this time.'

'Yes, Sister. What time is his appointment?'

'Eleven o'clock. The ambulance will pick you up on his rounds. By the way,' she smiled. 'Is that your little car in the garage?'

'Yes, I bought it at the weekend,' Nicola told her. 'I think it will come in very useful now that the winter is coming on. Geoff Carter found it for me. I was lucky to get one in such good condition.'

Sister patted her arm and smiled. 'I'm glad. You haven't been having a very nice time lately, have you? I was half afraid you might want to leave us after the unfortunate business with Natalie last week.'

'What I did was very foolish,' Nicola said. 'I should have known better.'

'Well I have to agree with you there,' Sister said frankly. 'But we all make mistakes, my dear, and you can't eat crow over it for evermore. You're a very good nurse and you have a good manner with this kind of patient. I've been cherishing fond hopes that when I retire—' She shrugged. 'Ah well, we must wait and see, mustn't we?'

'Natalie seems better this morning,' Nicola remarked.

'She is—thanks to Gerry Armstrong,' Sister told her. 'Do you know he's hardly left her side since it happened.' She patted Nicola's arm. 'The best thing we can all do is to try and forget about it as soon as we can.'

But Nicola was quite sure that she would never completely forget. Her heart still froze with horror whenever she thought about what might have happened.

The ambulance arrived on time and Nicola was waiting at the front door to help Gerry inside. As they sat side by side on the back seat she glanced at him.

'If everything goes well this morning you'll be leaving us soon, Gerry,' she said. 'Have you made any plans?'

He shrugged. 'Work and earning a living is the first priority. A mate of mine has offered me something. He has a garage, but I don't know if my legs will be up to the work yet.'

'I'm sure there will be plenty of things you can do

that won't entail long periods of standing,' she told him hopefully. 'If I were you I'd have a word with your doctor about it this morning. Anyway, it's great that you have an opportunity lined up.' She glanced at him sideways. 'We shall all miss you a lot, Gerry.'

He pulled a face. 'Oh don't worry. I shall be back to check up on all of you from time to time.'

'Coming back?' She looked at him in surprise. 'I thought you couldn't wait to see the back of Meadowlands.'

'Oh, you're not such a bad lot.' He frowned. 'To tell you the truth I'm not keen on leaving Natalie— that rotten business last week—'

It was out in the open at last and she was glad. 'It will be a long time before I can forgive myself for that,' she said with a sigh. 'If only I hadn't tried to play God.'

Gerry covered her hand with his own. 'Don't blame yourself, Staff. I know you meant well. I reckon I'd have done the same thing in your shoes. Anyway, maybe it's as well she found out about him while she was still at Meadowlands. It might have happened after she'd been discharged—when she was alone with no one to stop her doing it. Have you thought of that?'

She hadn't and it comforted her a little. She looked at Gerry. 'However you look at it, you saved her life,' she told him. 'Mine too in a way.'

He shook his head. 'Just luck—in more ways than one. She told me the whole story, poor kid. I know what it feels like to be ditched—made to feel like a reject. The same kind of thing happened to me, you know.'

She nodded. 'I'm sorry, Gerry.'

'I'm not!' he said angrily. 'There's nothing like a bit of trouble for sorting out who your friends are, as I told Natalie the other day.' He grinned wryly. 'You know, it's a funny thing to say, but this has done me a good turn in a way. I've always thought Natalie a fantastic girl but until now I've always been too shy to let her know.'

Nicola laughed. 'Shy! *You?* Gerry, you have to be joking!'

But he shook his head. 'No, really. You'd be surprised how bashful I am when it comes to something I feel deeply about.'

'And you feel deeply for Natalie?'

He coloured. 'Well, I—yes, I suppose you could say—oh damn it, I might as well come clean, seeing it's you, Staff. I'm in love with the girl, but you needn't tell everyone.'

'Of course I won't. What about Natalie, does she share your feelings?'

He pursed his lips. 'Maybe not yet, but I'm working on it,' he told her. 'It's funny. I wouldn't have stood a chance with a girl like her a few months ago. It's an ill wind, eh, Staff?'

While she was waiting for Gerry at the hospital she went in search of a cup of coffee. She found a machine at the end of the corridor and she was just turning away from it, cup in hand when she caught sight of Simon coming towards her. She looked around desperately, but there was no way to go except towards him and anyway, it was too late. He had already seen her.

'Good morning.'

She made a feeble attempt at surprise. 'Oh—good morning.'

'Why are you here—it isn't Natalie, is it?'

She shook her head. 'No, she's fine. I'm here with Gerry Armstrong. He's having his final check-up with Mr Devonish.'

'I see. That's good.' He paused, glancing round. There was no one else in sight. 'Did you enjoy your evening at the theatre?' he asked.

Her chin went up slightly. 'Very much, thank you.'

'Yes, you seemed to be enjoying yourself.'

There was an awkward pause which she broke by asking: 'How is Maria?'

'Very well. She started her new term today, so she won't be as much at a loose end as she was.'

His tone stung her. Was he trying to tell her that her company would no longer be required? 'That must be a relief for you,' she said crisply.

He nodded. 'I hear that we are to have your brother visiting later this week,' he said conversationally. 'I shall look forward to meeting him and seeing some of his work.'

She thought his choice of words patronising and she was about to make a sharp rejoinder when a door near them opened and a woman in a white coat came out. Nicola recognised her as Helen Frazer, Simon's companion at the theatre.

'Oh, good morning. I've been looking for you. Actually there's a case I rather wanted to discuss with you—' Helen Frazer looked pointedly at Nicola. 'But if you're too busy—'

'If you'll excuse me I believe my patient may be waiting by now.' Nicola turned and walked away towards the orthopaedic clinic. Her hands shook with anger as she sipped her half cold coffee. She was no longer in any doubt. She had been given the polite brush-off. Simon obviously had no further use for her.

Gerry came out of the clinic in high spirits. Mr Devonish, the orthopaedic surgeon was pleased with his progress and had promised that, subject to the result of the X-rays being as he hoped he could be discharged very soon. On the way back to Meadowlands in the ambulance he was full of plans.

'Natalie was telling me that she has kept her flat on,' he told her. 'And I've been thinking—I could open it up for her, couldn't I? Get it aired and cleaned and do any decorating she wants, ready for when she comes home.' He caught Nicola's expression and added quickly: 'I'd move out as soon as she came home, of course!' His look of boyish innocence made her laugh.

'Nothing like making yourself indispensable, is there? Gerry, you're about as subtle as a bulldozer!'

Natalie was waiting for the ambulance at the gate and when they climbed down Nicola saw the eagerness on her face as she took Gerry's arm, demanding to be told all about his check-up. When he told her she turned to Nicola, her eyes shining.

'Isn't that great news, Staff?'

'Marvellous.' Nicola took her other arm. 'Natalie, I've been meaning to have a talk with you—'

'Please—I know what you want to say but there's no need. It's I who should apologise for flaring up at you the way I did. Since it happened I've had time to think and I know now that I had to find out the truth about Rick some time. I'm just glad it came when it did. It gave me the chance to make some discoveries about myself.' As she said this Nicola noticed that she looked at Gerry and gave his arm a squeeze. If she didn't actually love him now it was obvious that the feeling between them would soon blossom. Nicola's relief was like a heavy burden being lifted from her shoulders.

Later, as she changed into a clean apron in her room, she reflected that they would soon be losing three patients. Gerry and Natalie would soon be discharged and Frank was due to start soon at the horticultural college in Gloucestershire. Three new places to be filled at Meadowlands—three new challenges to be met. She had learned a lot from the three who were leaving. She hoped she would be able to use her experience to help the newcomers.

Terry arrived on Wednesday evening and as soon as he was settled at Milton Green he drove over to Farthingbridge to see Nicola. She saw his large mobile workshop drive up from her window and hurried downstairs to meet him. As he jumped down from the van she saw that he looked tanned and healthy from a summer spent mostly in the open. His brown hair was streaked with gold and since she last saw him he had grown a beard. As she ran to meet him she called out:

'Terry! It's great to see you!'

He enveloped her in a bear-like hug, swinging her feet from the ground. 'Nicky! It seems ages since I saw my little sister. Well, how are you? Let's have a look at you.' He set her down and ran a critical, brotherly eye over her. 'Mmm—too skinny as usual—a bit peaky looking too. Don't like the look of you at all, in fact. Laura was saying you hadn't been quite yourself lately.'

'Thanks a lot,' Nicola said dryly. 'You always did know how to make a girl feel special!'

He laughed. 'Sorry, love. Seriously though, you do look as though you could do with a break. Been finding the work here hard going?'

She shrugged noncommittally. 'Oh—you know what it's like—getting broken into a new job. This work is very different from intensive care.' She glanced sideways at him, wondering just how much Laura had told him, but he didn't press her further.

'Well, you know what I always say,' he said cheerfully. 'Be your own boss; make your own hours and enjoy the sunshine while it's there!'

She smiled and took his arm. 'Come in and meet the patients,' she invited. 'They're looking forward so much to your talk and concert tomorrow evening.'

'Is there anyone here who might be a likely candidate for a trainee?' he asked as they walked.

'I don't know.' She looked at him thoughtfully. 'Why do you ask?'

'Well, to begin with I'm getting quite a few orders for instruments,' he told her. 'I believe my work could snowball into something quite important and I really should train someone to carry it on. I think a disabled person would be ideal. He could help to show others what can be done from a wheelchair.'

Nicola smiled delightedly. 'I think that's a wonderful idea. And I'm glad you're doing so well.'

He slipped an arm round her shoulders and hugged her. 'Ah well, you're not the only one in the family with brains, you know. I'm not just the pretty one!'

She laughed and jabbed him playfully in the ribs just as Gerry and Natalie came round the corner hand in hand. Nicola made quick introductions and Terry looked at the pair frankly.

'If you don't mind my saying so you two aren't at all my idea of patients,' he said. 'You look like a couple of frauds to me!'

Gerry laughed. 'Well, we are just about ready to leave. You should have seen us when we first came, eh, Staff? If we look like frauds now it's all down to marvellous people like your sister here.'

Nicola blushed with pleasure. 'And the support you give to each other,' she said. 'Don't forget that.'

Sister Martin had arranged a special tea for Terry the following afternoon in her office. She seemed to take to Terry on sight. He pulled her leg outrageously which she seemed to enjoy and by the time the light meal was over the mood was well and truly set for the evening to come. It was while Nicola was changing that her telephone rang and at first she didn't recognise the childish voice at the other end of the line:

'Nicola—is that you? It's me, Maria.'

'Maria. Is anything wrong?' The child sounded upset.

'I wanted to know if it's true what Daddy says, that you're not coming to our house any more.'

Nicola was shocked and for a moment at a loss for words. 'You and I are friends, Maria,' she said after a moment. 'I'm here whenever you want me.'

'But why won't you come here any more?'

'I haven't said that—' Nicola racked her brain to think of a way to explain to the child the awkwardness between Simon and herself. 'Look—we're having a concert here this evening. I think your daddy is coming. Why don't you ask him to bring you too?'

'I have, but he won't. I'm back at school now and everything is horrible—' She was in tears now and Nicola's heart ached for her. How could Simon be so unkind? Was he really mean enough to take out his anger with her on Maria?

'Don't cry, darling,' she said. 'I'll come and see you again just as soon as I can. Don't worry. I won't let you down.'

'Promise?' Maria whispered.

'I promise.' As she replaced the receiver Nicola was fuming. She had always thought Simon such a good father. How could he treat his daughter like this?

Everyone had dressed up for the evening's entertainment and the atmosphere in the large lounge was quite festive. Sister Martin had brought her husband along and most of the care assistants were there too. Ted and Marjorie were to serve a special buffet half way through the evening and they were both there in the audience, looking forward to hearing Staff Nurse Page's talented brother.

He had brought a selection of his hand-made instruments, guitars, dulcimers and small table harps. There was even a lute, his latest venture. The first half of the evening was given to Terry's entertaining story of how he came to be interested in music as therapy and how he came to teach himself to play and to make the instruments. He had brought some of his tools and samples of the wood he used and he told them about the far-away places where it grew—the rain forests and jungles where the temperature and humidity are just right. He made them laugh with stories of some of his adventures on the road and brought tears to their eyes when he told of disabled children who had given up until they found joy again in creating music. Nicola, who had been sitting near the back of the room, saw Simon come in quietly soon after Terry had begun speaking. She watched him out of the corner of her eye as he found an empty chair and sat down. Feeling her eyes on him he looked across and for a moment his gaze held hers. Her heart contracted. He looked tired and unhappy and

she longed to go to him and put her hand in his.
Then she remembered Maria's tearful voice on the
telephone earlier and hardened her heart, turning
again to give her attention to Terry.

When his lecture was at an end she rose to help
Marjorie with the refreshments. The talk had gone
down well and everyone wanted to speak to Terry
during the break, especially Jim. Nicola had
noticed the interest in his face during the time that
Terry was speaking and now, as she dispensed
coffee she saw that, with Terry's help he was trying
out one of the guitars. As she passed close to them
she heard to her surprise that he could play quite
well and she was pleased to see that he and Terry
were getting along famously together.

'Nicola, can I talk to you?' She turned as she
felt a hand on her arm, her heart quickening as
she found herself looking into Simon's eyes.
She looked around, searching her mind for an
excuse.

'I—I'm rather busy at the moment.'

He took the tray firmly out of her hands. 'I don't
think you are. Everyone seems to have something
to eat and drink at the moment. Come out into the
garden.'

Someone had opened the french windows to let
in the cool evening air and Nicola followed Simon
out through them, her mind refusing to offer a
reasonable excuse not to. His hand under her
elbow he led her to the far end of the terrace where
the angle of two walls made a secluded corner.

'Nicola—' She felt her heart melt as his eyes

looked down into hers. 'I'm sorry I was so harsh with you over Natalie.'

She shook her head. 'No, you were quite right.'

'I was angry about the setback I felt sure she would suffer,' he went on. 'But I seem to have been wrong about that.'

'There really wasn't any need for you to apologise to me.' She began to walk away but he reached out to put his hands on her shoulders.

'It wasn't just that. I have to admit that I was pretty shattered by the row we had. I had no right—no right at all to allow it to affect our working relationship though. That was unforgivable.' He put a finger under her chin so that he could look into her eyes. 'I hope you'll accept my apology.'

'Of course.' She looked up at him. 'Why did you tell Maria that I wouldn't be seeing her again?'

He frowned. 'How did you know that?'

'She telephoned me. She was terribly upset. I'm sure she felt I'd let her down. You had no right to give her that impression.'

He shook his head. 'There is still a very great deal you don't understand, Nicola. Maria has had some severe setbacks in her short life. They've affected her badly. I didn't want to risk any more disappointments for her.'

'Surely you didn't imagine that I'd do anything to hurt Maria,' she reproached him.

'Not knowingly. I thought it might be awkward for you if you wanted to avoid seeing me. I did it to save you embarrassment.'

She turned away from him. 'Perhaps Maria will

get to like Dr Helen Frazer just as much in time!' As soon as she had said it she bit her lip in dismay. It sounded so bitchy and small-minded.

His eyes darkened. 'If you really want to know, I ran into Helen quite by chance the other evening at the theatre. Not that you deserve an explanation after a remark like that,' he said icily.

She turned away. 'It doesn't matter to me how you met her!'

He caught her arm angrily. 'At least I didn't make an exhibition of myself in public!' His eyes glowered furiously into hers, his fingers biting into her arm painfully.

'You're hurting me—let me go. My life is—' She broke off as she caught sight of someone coming towards them along the terrace.

'Hi, Nicola. Sorry I'm late. I almost didn't make it. Someone said you were out here. I—Oh, good evening, Mr Grey.' Geoff stood looking awkwardly from one to the other, painfully aware that he had interrupted something.

Simon looked at Nicola. 'I'll leave you, then. Perhaps you have unfinished business to attend to.' And without a glance in Geoff's direction he strode off, leaving them both staring speechlessly after him.

Geoff let out a long slow breath. 'Phew—trust me! I'm sorry, Nicola. Did I barge in at the wrong moment?' She shook her head unhappily, unable to trust herself to speak. Geoff frowned. 'Anyway, what did he mean about "unfinished business"?'

She sighed 'I don't know.' She forced herself to

smile at him. 'Shall we go inside now, Geoff? Terry must be ready to begin the second half of his programme.'

The rest of the evening was to be devoted to an informal concert with Terry demonstrating his skill on the various instruments he had brought. His audience was enthralled. He played everything from 'pop' to classics with a sprinkling of medieval and folk music but right at the end of his programme he sprung a surprise on Nicola.

'I'd like to end the evening by playing a great favourite of mine,' he announced. 'It also happens to be a favourite of my sister's and one she used to sing along with me when we were both students, so I'm going to ask her to step up here and sing it with me now.' He held out a hand to her. 'Come on, Nicola, Scarborough Fair.'

Nicola blushed and shook her head as all heads turned to look at her and smile encouragement. 'No—really, I can't,' she said. But Terry was not to be so easily put off. Getting up from his stool he came into the audience to fetch her, much to everyone's delight. Silently vowing to have her own back later she followed him reluctantly. Simon seemed to have left after their conversation during the interval and now she was glad. At least he wasn't here to see her make a fool of herself again!

Terry played the introduction while she took a deep breath, praying that she could remember the words, but as they began to sing together the significance of the lyrics got through to her, lending a sweet huskiness to her voice that made Terry look at her with a slight raising of his eyebrows. She was just coming to the last line when something caught her attention. Out of the corner of her eye she saw that someone stood on the terrace, outside the french windows. She turned and saw Maria, her dark eyes huge in a white face as she stared fixedly in at Terry and her. As the last notes of the guitar died away Terry stood up and slipped an arm round Nicola, kissing her on the cheek as the delighted audience broke into applause. Maria's mouth opened in a silent cry and she disappeared from view, vanishing into the darkness beyond the terrace.

With a sense of urgency Nicola made a hurried excuse and left the room. Every instinct told her that something was wrong—badly wrong. In the hall she met Marjorie. 'Did you see Maria?' she asked. 'She was out there on the terrace. I saw her just now.'

'I saw her leaving,' Marjorie said. 'On her bike. Going as if the hounds of hell were after her. I was looking out of the landing window and—'

'Which way did she go?' Nicola interrupted. 'Did she go across the park—towards home?'

Marjorie frowned. 'Now that you mention it, no, she didn't. She went down the drive.'

Nicola's heart had begun to beat fast. What was it that had upset the child so much? Was she so desperate she'd try to run away? She opened the door. 'I'm going after her in the car,' she told Marjorie over her shoulder. 'If anyone asks where I am make some excuse for me, will you?'

'But it's raining—you'll get wet!' Marjorie called after her. But she didn't hear, already she was running towards the garage, hardly noticing the heavy drops of cold rain on her bare arms and neck.

CHAPTER ELEVEN

She was just driving out of the garage when Geoff caught her up. She wound down the window.

'I'm going after Maria,' she called. 'I saw her through the window and she seemed to be upset about something.'

He nodded. 'I saw her too. I guessed where you were going when I saw you leaving. Mrs Shelford thought you might need these.' He handed her a blanket and a torch. 'Do you want me to come with you?'

'Thanks, but no. I think it's better if I go alone. I'd be grateful if you'd ring her father though. He may not even know she's missing. Tell him to stay put until he hears from me. If I find her I'll take her straight home. She can't have gone far.'

He stood back. 'I'll do it at once. Take care.'

As she urged the car forward down the drive it began to rain heavily. Maria hadn't been wearing a coat. She'd soon be wet through. She switched on the windscreen wipers, straining her eyes into the darkness along the headlights' beam. All around her stretched the open heathland, bleak and desolate. Heavy dark clouds hid the moon and stars and there was no sound except for the drumming of the rain on the car roof and the rhythmic swish of the

wipers. Nowhere could she see any sign of a child
on a cycle. If she had stopped to shelter she could
be anywhere. It was like looking for a needle in a
haystack. Then she had a sudden thought—Pixie
Lake! Could she have gone there? There was certainly more shelter and it seemed to be a place that
Maria felt drawn to. When she came to the narrow
track she turned off the road and nosed the car
carefully through what was now a sea of sandy mud
which the car churned into a quagmire. Nicola
prayed that her hunch would prove to be right; if
she were to get bogged down in this hidden track
for nothing it could be disastrous.

In the rain and dark the place was eerier than
ever. Nicola positioned the car so that the headlights would illuminate the place a little. Even in
this light the water was blue—a dark, inky blue that
was somehow menacing. The steep sides of the pit
gave the place a claustrophobic feel and she shud-
dered, wishing she'd let Geoff come with her after
all.

For a moment she stood shivering, arms wrapped
round herself while the rain soaked into the thin
material of her dress. What should she do—where
should she start looking? Then she thought she saw
a shape huddling in the shelter of the overhanging
bushes. Going back to the car she switched off the
headlights, realising that if she wasn't careful she'd
find herself with a flat battery. Reaching into the
dark interior she found the torch that Geoff had
given her. It might be nothing—a shadow or a trick
of the light, even a sheltering animal, but whatever

it was she didn't want to frighten it off until she'd had a chance to find out.

Her feet sank into the wet sand as she made her way across the tiny beach, shining the torch towards the place where she had seen the shape. Tentatively she called: 'Maria are you there? Don't be afraid—it's me—Nicola.' She fancied she heard a sound—a faint whimper and she stopped to listen. It came from quite close to where she stood and again she shone the torch.

She hardly recognised the small figure who recoiled from her, eyes narrowed against the glare of the light. She was soaked to the skin, her dark hair matted by the wind and rain, clinging to her face and neck in string-like strands. With a gasp Nicola sank to her knees in the mud beside her.

'Maria, darling! What are you doing here? Why did you run away like that? What was it that frightened you so? Tell me.'

But the child seemed unable to speak. Teeth chattering she collapsed against Nicola, silent sobs shaking her thin shoulders. Without another word Nicola picked her up and carried her across to the car. Opening the door she pulled out the blanket, grateful for Marjorie's presence of mind, and wrapped it firmly round the shivering child, bundling her into the passenger seat and climbing in beside her. She was obviously suffering from a mixture of exposure and shock and she wished she had something hot to drink with her. The best thing she could do was to get her home as soon as possible. She slipped an arm round her.

'I'm going to take you home to Daddy now. Are you all right?'

Maria shook her head. 'No, I don't want to go home—' She forced the words past her clenched teeth. 'Not yet, Nicola, please!'

'But I must get you home. You need a hot bath and dry clothes. Daddy will be worried about you too. You don't want that, do you?'

'He'll be so angry when he knows—it's just like it was that other time—you don't understand. It was my fault—I remember now—*my* fault!' She shook her head from side to side, tears pouring down her cheeks, almost hysterical. 'I knew when I heard it, you see.' She looked at Nicola with terrified eyes. 'I always knew I'd hear something one day that would make me remember the thing I'd forgotten.'

Nicola was afraid herself now. She took Maria by the shoulders and held her firmly. 'Tell me what you heard—and what it was you remembered. You must tell me. I can't help unless you do.'

Maria took a deep breath and seemed to control herself a little. 'It was the song—the one you were singing—with the man.'

Nicola frowned. 'Scarborough Fair?'

The child nodded. 'It was what *he* used to play.'

Nicola thought she'd go mad with frustration. 'Who, Maria—*who*?'

'His name was Ross—' Maria frowned as the tangled threads of her memory slowly unravelled. 'He was Mummy's friend, and he played the guitar too. Sometimes he'd be on the television—singing that same song.' She swallowed hard, biting her lip.

Nicola picked up one small cold hand and began to rub it.

'Take your time,' she said gently. 'Tell me what happened.'

'It was when we lived at Meadowlands—a long time ago. It was raining that night too. I thought at first it was the rain that woke me, then I knew that it was Ross and Mummy downstairs. They were arguing—shouting at each other. I was frightened. I crept downstairs to listen and I saw Mummy's case and all her things in the hall. I guessed then that she was going away. The door was open and I could see them. Mummy was saying that she wasn't letting Daddy have me but Ross said he didn't want to take me too. He said, "Kids are bad news—bad—"' she furrowed her brow in concentration—' "bad *vibes*. Take her and it's all up between us".'

Nicola studied the small face. It was as though she was hearing that night's conversation all over again. Obviously she couldn't have known at the time what the man Ross meant and yet she remembered every word—every phrase exactly. With a feeling of horror in the pit of her stomach Nicola began to understand the tragic situation that had cost Maria the innocence of her childhood two years ago.

'What did you do, darling?' she probed softly.

Maria looked at her. Her eyes were calmer now and she had almost stopped shaking. 'I was afraid. I didn't want Mummy to leave us—I couldn't let her go without me so I crept outside and got into the car. I sat on the floor in the back and covered myself with a rug. I knew it was naughty, but I thought that Mummy would be pleased and maybe when he saw me Ross wouldn't take her away after all.' Her lower lip began to tremble again and she caught it between her teeth. 'Then it happened—'

'What happened? Tell me, Maria. If you do the hurt will go away.'

'I got hot and itchy in the back of the car. I thought it was time to let them know I was there so I popped up. Ross was very angry. He shouted and turned round—the car skidded. It went off the road and turned over and over. I could hear Mummy screaming and then there was nothing until I woke up in the hospital.' She looked at Nicola. 'It was back there—' She pointed back along the track towards the road. So *that* was why the child was so drawn to this place. Nicola held her close.

'It's all right, darling. You're all right now.'

'But now I know that it was my fault that Mummy died!' Maria whispered. 'How can I tell Daddy? What will he say when he knows?'

'Nothing was your fault. You mustn't say that— you mustn't even think it,' Nicola told her as she rocked her, trying to warm and comfort her. So many things were clear to her now. Maria's revelation was like the last piece of a puzzle. On the night she died Claudia had been leaving Simon for another man. That was why he couldn't live at Meadowlands any more. The memories were too traumatic. She settled Maria back in her seat.

'I'm going to drive you home now. A hot bath

and a good night's sleep and you'll be as good as new,' she said.

Maria looked at her. 'Nicola—you're not going away too are you—with the man you were singing with? You're not going to—to *marry* him, are you?'

Nicola stared at her in surprise. 'Of course not! That was my brother, Terry. Don't you remember me telling you about him?'

The child's face cleared. 'Oh—yes, I see.' She squeezed Nicola's hand. 'You won't ever go away, will you, Nicola?' she begged.

Nicola sighed as she switched on the ignition and eased the car into reverse. Before long it was inevitable that Maria would be hurt again. There seemed no way of avoiding it. But for tonight at least she must shelve the problem. 'No—I won't go away,' she said weakly.

The front door of the Dower House was open, yellow light from the hall flooding welcomingly into the garden. As she slammed the door of the Mini Simon came out, followed closely by a relieved looking Mrs Dickens. Nicola helped Maria out.

'Can you walk?' she asked, but Simon was already there, scooping his daughter up into his arms and carrying her inside quickly. Nicola looked at Mrs Dickens.

'I found her at the place she calls Pixie Lake. Something had triggered off her memory of the night her mother was killed,' she explained.

The woman nodded. 'I'm not surprised. The other day when she asked you to take her there I wondered how long it would be before she remembered. It was always a favourite place of hers. Her mother painted a picture of it for her. It used to hang in her bedroom, but Mr Grey had it taken down after the accident.' She looked gratefully at Nicola. 'I can't tell you how relieved I am that she's found. I felt so responsible. It was just like that other terrible night all over again. Thank you, Miss Page.' She laid a hand on Nicola's arm and exclaimed at the state of her dress. 'You're wet through too. Please come in and let me get you something.'

But Nicola shook her head. 'I'll be getting back, thank you all the same. My brother will be wondering where I've got to.' As she was getting into the car she remembered something. 'Oh—Maria's bike! It's still there at the lake. Perhaps you could send someone to get it tomorrow.'

'I will, but won't you change your mind and stay? I know Mr Grey will want to thank you.'

Nicola switched on the ignition. 'It's rather late. I'd better go.' She couldn't face Simon tonight—not now that she knew the truth. 'I'll ring tomorrow to see how Maria is,' she called as she turned the car. 'Goodnight.'

By the time she got back to Meadowlands everyone had retired for the night but Terry was waiting for her in her flat. As soon as she walked in he got up from his chair with a smothered exclamation and went into the bathroom to run her a bath.

'Get those wet things off at once,' he ordered. 'I'll get you a hot drink. Have you got any brandy?' She shook her head as she kicked off her ruined shoes and he tut-tutted at her, shaking his head.

'Call yourself a nurse! When it comes to looking after yourself you're no better than a babe in arms!'

She felt decidedly better after her bath and as she sat in front of the electric fire clutching the mug of hot chocolate that Terry had made for her she caught him looking quizzically at her.

'I don't suppose you'd care to tell me what all this is about?' he asked.

She affected a look of surprise. 'A child ran away—I went after her. What more is there to know?'

He pulled a face. 'Come off it, Nick. To begin with Maria Grey isn't just *any* child and to follow, what scared her and why did it have to be *you* who went haring off after her?'

She sighed wearily. 'Give it a rest now, Terry. I'm too tired to go into it at the moment.'

He bent forward to touch her hand lightly. 'You know, I'd been wondering why the name rang a bell, then I remembered. Simon Grey was the guy you were so besotted with when you were training at Bishop's Wood, wasn't he?' She looked away and he went on: 'And he's married. Don't tell me you're still carrying that particular torch?'

She got up from her chair angrily. 'I'm not going to discuss it with you, Terry. I'll just tell you this: Simon Grey's wife was killed in a car accident two years ago. Maria was involved too. Tonight she came over here to hear you play and our singing the song Scarborough Fair triggered off the memory of that traumatic night. I guessed where she might have gone and I was right. Now she's home and safe.' She turned to look at him defiantly. 'Does that satisfy your curiosity?'

He ignored her edginess. 'And what about you—are you all right?' he asked quietly.

'Yes—*yes*! For God's sake leave me alone, Terry!' she exploded. 'I'm tired out and I have to be on duty early tomorrow morning. Look—I'll be over to see you tomorrow evening as soon as I come off duty. All right?'

He got up and stood for a moment, looking down into her anguished face. 'If you say so.' He ruffled her damp curly hair affectionately. 'Thanks for asking me to Meadowlands, Nick. I like it here. Sleep well—hope you feel better in the morning—'night.'

He closed the door softly and she felt the lump in her throat swell unbearably. She hadn't meant to snap at him but after the tension of the past hours his searching questions were more than she could bear. Tomorrow she would give in her notice and set about looking for a new job. Then she would have to go and see Maria—try to explain to the child why it was impossible for her to stay—hope she wouldn't be too upset.

'Will you sit down, please, Nicola?' It was the first time that Sister Martin had ever used her Christian name. Nicola closed the office door and sat down on the opposite side of the desk. Sister looked at her.

'Would you like to tell me—in confidence, of course—why it is that you wish to leave?'

Nicola shook her head. 'It's personal—nothing to do with the work here. I've been very happy in that respect.'

'We need you very badly at the moment, you know.' Sister looked up. 'Three new patients are to be admitted next week. You'd be leaving just as they were getting used to you.' There was a pause while Nicola looked helplessly at her hands, folded in her lap. How could she possibly explain how intolerable it would be for her to stay after all that had happened?

'I believe I've guessed what the trouble is,' Sister said gently. 'Though of course it's really none of my business. But I'd like you to know that if there's anything at all I can do to help you have only to ask.'

Nicola shook her head, her cheeks colouring. 'There's nothing anyone can do,' she said miserably. 'But it's very kind of you to want to help.'

'I'm selfish really,' Sister smiled. 'I don't want to lose a good nurse.' When Nicola still seemed at a loss for words she leaned across the desk. 'Look— yesterday was your day off but you spent most of your time working hard, helping to get ready for your brother's entertainment. We're not busy at the moment so why don't you run along and spend the day with him? He told me he would be at Milton Green until Sunday. Get right away from Meadow-lands and think things through.'

Nicola shrugged. 'I'm better working. Thinking doesn't seem to help.'

'Go anyway. The break will do you good. You know you're looking very peaky.' Sister patted her hand. 'If you won't let me help why don't you ask your brother's advice? He seemed to me to be a very understanding young man and I'm sure he's fond of you.'

Nicola stood up. 'I appreciate your kindness Sister, and a day off would be nice. But I'm afraid I can't promise to change my mind.'

'Well, if you can't, you can't.' Sister got up and opened the door for her. 'Have a day's relaxation anyway.'

In her flat Nicola changed out of her uniform and into a tweed skirt and soft cashmere sweater. It would be good to get away and be with Terry. She felt so tired—as though, given the peace of mind she could sleep for a week.

When she arrived at the cottage Laura was at work and the door was opened to her by Terry. He wore his dressing gown and his hair was tousled. The expression of surprise on his face was almost comical.

'Nicky! What's up? You're not ill or anything, are you?'

She smiled. 'Some of us actually get up at a reasonable hour in the morning! Sister gave me the day off and suggested I spent it with you.'

In the kitchen he poured her a cup of the strong coffee he had just made while the dogs fussed round her feet, jostling each other for her attention. 'Is there any particular reason for her giving you this time off?' he asked, eyeing her suspiciously.

She shrugged. 'You seem to have made a hit with her. She didn't like thinking of you here all alone.'

'I may be male and chauvinist but I don't buy *that*!' he said. 'Now tell me the real reason.'

'No mystery. She just thought I needed a day off.'

'Why?'

'What do you mean—*why*?' She coloured, unable to keep up the pretence under his candid stare. 'Oh all right—if you must know, I gave in my notice this morning. She thought I ought to have time to think it over.'

'You gave in your notice! Why?'

Her eyes flashed at him. 'If you say "why" once more I shall hit you with that coffee pot! I don't want to work at Meadowlands any more, that's all. I don't cross examine *you* about what you do with your life, so don't start on me!'

He sat down on a kitchen stool, looking at her speculatively, completely unmoved by her outburst of temper. 'I'd say that something had been getting you down,' he said calmly. 'Something or *someone*. It doesn't do to bottle things up, you know, Nick. Why don't you tell me all about it? I was right last night, wasn't I? It *is* this Simon Grey?' She gave in, nodding miserably and he poured her another cup of coffee.

'You say he's a widower now,' he said thoughtfully. 'If he's free what's the problem? Is it that the feeling is all on one side?'

She shook her head, wishing he'd leave the subject alone. It felt like having an open wound probed. With unsteady hands she reached for her cup, folding her fingers round it to keep them from trembling.

'He asked me to marry him, Terry. But I'm pretty sure it was only because he needed a mother for his daughter.'

Terry's eyebrows rose. 'I can't see why you should think that. You're not bad looking—a lot younger than him too. You're even a fairly good cook! I think he'd be lucky to get you!'

She sighed impatiently. How could Sister Martin have thought Terry 'understanding'? 'It isn't as simple as that, Terry—Simon's first wife was everything I'm not—beautiful, talented, brilliantly accomplished. Anyone he marries now would rate a poor second. I don't want to be second best— especially not to Simon.'

'So—if you can't be his first choice you'd rather be nothing—give him up?' He looked at her pityingly. 'I'm sorry but I think that's feeble.'

Nicola got up from the table and began to wash the cups at the sink to hide her impatience. 'This conversation is getting us nowhere, Terry. Can we change the subject?'

'You seem pretty mixed up to me,' he told her. 'Maybe you *should* talk about it. Surely you wouldn't let it spoil things for you—make you give up a job that you really like? That's a bit over the top, isn't it? We all have disappointments—look at me—'

She spun round to him. 'Oh shut up, Terry! There are other things—things you don't know about—that I can't tell you. I feel that Simon chose me for all the wrong reasons, because of not being beautiful or any of the things that Claudia was.'

He frowned. 'Is that so bad?'

'Oh *Terry*!' She was almost in tears now. 'Can't you understand—I want him to *love* me. I want him to marry me because he can't bear not to—because I'm the one person in the whole world he wants to be with—not just because I happen to fit neatly into an empty slot in his life!' She threw down the teatowel she had been drying the cups with. 'Oh! I might as well go back to Meadowlands if this is the way it's going to be!'

He caught her arm as she was halfway through the door. 'Hey—don't go like that. Poor Nick, you really have got it bad, haven't you? Calm down, love. I do understand, you know.'

Kind words were the last straw. With a choking sob she buried her head against his shoulder.

'That's right—' He patted her back comfortingly. 'Have a good cry. I told you it was bad to bottle it all up. Let it all go and then we'll go out and treat ourselves to a slap-up lunch and to hell with the rest of the world, eh?'

Terry was right, she did feel better after a good cry and when she had washed her face and made it up again upstairs in her old room they set off in the Mini with the dogs, determined to enjoy the rest of the day together in the old, light-hearted way they used to. But try as she would Nicola couldn't shake off the feeling of nostalgia. It seemed to her that everything she saw and did was for the last time. Even the weather seemed to be having a last fling after last night's storm. The late September sun gave everything an exotic, almost too brilliant sparkle that gave the scenery a picture-postcard look.

They drove down to Lulworth and when they caught their first glimpse of the sea Nicola saw that it was smooth and calm. 'Like the smile on the face of the tiger' she told herself. In a few weeks it would lash and roar, throwing itself at the craggy cliffs in a fury, as though it wanted to destroy everything in sight. But she wouldn't be here to see it. She sighed. By then she would be far away, maybe in the North of England again—away from the sea and the Forest—away from Meadowlands and from Simon, this time for ever.

She tried hard to enjoy the delicious lunch that Terry insisted on ordering for her, choosing all the things he knew she liked, including her favourite wine. Over coffee he told her that he was going to offer Jim a job.

'If things go well I want to set up a workshop and train people to make my instruments,' he explained. 'And I'd like to employ disabled workers. I've got my eye on a large house that I hope to convert so that they can live in as well. I'm hoping that there's some kind of grant I can apply for so that I can fix it up with all the equipment they'd need to be independent. The idea is that we'd all help and support each other. I've been talking about it to Laura and to your nice Sister Martin and they're both quite keen on the idea. Jim is to be the first—a sort of guinea-pig, if he agrees—to see how it works out. What do you think of the idea, Nick?'

She looked up at him. 'Oh Terry—I think it's a *super* idea! You must have been dying to talk about it all day and all I could do was to go on and on about my own problems.'

His good-natured grin reappeared and he patted her hand. 'Never mind. I'm going to have to get used to sharing other people's problems, aren't I? Maybe I've lived for myself and by myself far too long anyway.'

They walked on the beach after lunch, climbing the rocks and exploring the caves they had loved as children. The dogs enjoyed themselves too, chasing gulls and racing up and down the sand after sticks. But although they laughed a lot Nicola couldn't throw off the feeling of bittersweet sadness. She was just wondering how she would tackle the task of telling Maria that she was leaving when Terry called to her:

'Time to go! Tide's coming in!'

She looked up and realised for the first time that a chilly breeze had sprung up with the turn of the tide. She shivered. The day was almost at an end. She took the hand her brother held out to her and, whistling to the dogs, they climbed the steep path to the place where they had left the car.

By the time they reached Milton Green again

they were both longing for a cup of tea. Nicola drove the Mini straight into the drive and they saw that Laura's car was in the garage. Terry remarked that with a bit of luck she'd have the kettle on. Glancing at Nicola's pensive face he called as he got out of the car:

'Come on, lazy! Race you to the back door!'

It was a game they had played as children and she responded automatically, taking off at speed round the side of the cottage towards the kitchen door, the dogs hot on her heels.

'Hey! That's not fair—you had a head start!' Terry called after her, but she ignored him, almost falling over Laura's potted geraniums as she pushed open the door and threw herself breathlessly into the kitchen. Inside she stopped short and Terry cannoned into her. He jostled her, pushing her out of the way.

'What's the matter? You almost—Oh!' He followed Nicola's gaze. Laura sat at the kitchen table. She was not alone and it was her visitor who had brought Nicola up short. She stared at him, her cheeks drained of colour and the laughter dying on her lips. He was pale too, his eyes grave as they held hers across the room.

'Hello, Nicola,' Simon said.

CHAPTER TWELVE

IN THE few seconds that they stared at each other Nicola took in every detail of the scene before her. Simon sat opposite Laura at the kitchen table. Between them, a pot of tea and two cups—an untouched plate of biscuits. It was obvious from their faces that they had been talking seriously. Had Laura been giving him 'piece of her mind'? He wore casual clothes, slacks and a polo neck sweater; he was slightly—very slightly in need of a shave and his usually groomed hair was ruffled as though he had spent the day out of doors. Why was it that these things tugged so painfully at her heart? She came to her senses as Laura stood up and gave Terry a meaning look.

'Terry, I'm glad you're back. There's a little job I want you to do for me—upstairs.' She opened the hall door and beckoned to him. For a moment Terry hesitated, looking hard at Nicola's white face, then, reluctantly he followed Laura who closed the door firmly behind them.

Simon stood up and came towards her. 'I've been trying to track you down all day. I wanted to thank you for what you did last night.'

She shook her head. 'It was nothing—just lucky that I happened to think of the lake. How is Maria, by the way?'

'She's fine. Nicola—' He reached out to touch her but she shrank away. If he touched her now she would be lost and she had never needed strength as much as she did at this moment. He went on: 'When I went to Meadowlands this morning Sister Martin told me that you'd given in your notice.'

'That's right.'

For a moment he looked mutely at her, then he said: 'Please—don't go.'

The inflection he used and his eyes as they looked into hers strained her resolve almost to breaking point. She felt like a sheet of metal passed through a white hot flame—melting, softening. Taking a deep breath she turned to look out of the window, avoiding his eyes.

'Natalie's troubles seem to be over. I think the damage I did has been put right, even though I can't take the credit for it. There's nothing left to stay for.'

'Isn't there, Nicola?' He took her by the shoulders and turned her to face him. '*Isn't* there?'

She tried to avoid the grey eyes but it was impossible as they burned into hers. 'Maria, you mean?' she whispered.

'You know damned well I don't mean Maria!' His voice was ragged and the hands that gripped her shoulders tightened. 'You know, of course, that last night Maria remembered the circumstances of her mother's death. When she was in bed—after the shock had lessened a little she wanted to talk. There were questions she wanted to ask—painful ones, the answers to which I'd kept suppressed for far too long. Once I tried to talk to you about it but at the last minute my nerve failed me. I thought if you knew the truth you might be put off and you were too important to me to risk that.' He dropped his hands to his sides. 'Will you listen now while I tell you about it, Nicola? I think we owe each other that.'

'Yes, Simon. I'll listen,' she said quietly.

He took her arm. 'Not here. I left my car at the end of the lane. We'll drive somewhere. It may take some time.'

She hesitated. 'I'd better tell Laura.' But he shook his head.

'She'll know. We talked for a while before you came home. She'll understand.'

They drove in silence. Once or twice Nicola looked at his profile. His mouth was set in a tight line and tension showed in every muscle—even in his hands on the wheel. She longed to put her arms around him and kiss away the pain she saw in his eyes but she held her emotions in check. If she kissed him now she wouldn't hear a word he said.

When at last they drew up she saw that they were at the same hilltop where they had come on the night Simon had proposed. It looked very different in daylight. She watched the small boats bobbing in the bay below, their white sails like pieces of paper tossed in the wind. Simon switched off the engine and turned to her.

'Shall we stay here or would you like to walk?'

She was tired—more tired than she ever remembered being but she knew she couldn't stay this close to Simon and think straight. 'I think I'd like to walk,' she said, opening the car door.

There was a winding path leading through the trees down into the chine. It was still slightly muddy from last night's rain, here and there knotted with ancient tree roots. As they walked he made no attempt to touch her.

'Claudia was beautiful,' he began slowly. 'But of course you knew that—everyone did. What many people didn't know was that she was hard under all that beauty; brittle, demanding and hard—not a softness anywhere about her. You can see it in her pictures. They have genius—a great talent, but no compassion, no sensitivity. I put them all away—afterwards. Perhaps I should sell them and put the money in trust for Maria. I think that would be the best—'

It was almost as though he were talking to himself and she let him go on, sensing that what he had to say would take time.

'She never loved me. To be fair I don't think she was capable of love,' he went on. 'She used her beauty as a fisherman uses bait—to catch what she wanted, but her weakness was that she could never bear to throw back any of the poor fish she caught. I realised very early that our marriage was a terrible mistake. All she wanted was the money I'd inherited and the status of being a consultant's wife. But the life disappointed her. It was far too dull and she certainly didn't want to hear about my work. To her sickness of any kind was obscene. Ross Barrett was the last of a long string of affairs. He was a pop-singer—the leader of a folk group. Most of the men she took up with were from that kind of background and none of them cared two hoots about her, but then that was the way she wanted it. To her lovers were a disposable commodity—like paper cups—something to be used and tossed aside.' He sighed deeply. 'Why she decided to go away with Ross Barrett I'll never know.'

'Was he killed too on the night of the crash?' Nicola asked.

'No. Ironically he escaped with a few scratches. He was desperate to keep the whole thing quiet— something to do with his "image" being damaged. As you can guess I wasn't anxious for a sordid scandal either. Afterwards he went to America. I haven't a clue what happened to him.'

She glanced at him, trying to assess just how much all this was hurting. 'It must all have been very painful for you,' she ventured. 'After all, she was your wife and you loved her.'

He sighed. 'I fell in love with her beauty—as so many others did. I was dazzled by her. She used to laugh at the way she'd taken me in—taunt me with her affairs. She threatened that if I ever tried to divorce her she'd have all of it spread across the gossip sheets. I didn't care for myself, but with Maria growing up I was afraid of what it might do to her. I thought I was doing the right thing for her by living out that sham.' He gave a bitter little laugh. 'Little did I know what I was storing up for the child!'

Nicola looked at him, unable to bear the anguish

in his voice any longer. 'Please, don't blame your-self—' Her foot caught in a tree root and she stumbled. He caught at her arm.

'Are you all right?'

'Yes—' She steadied herself and looked up into his eyes. His hand on her arm was warm, making her flesh tingle. 'Yes—' she whispered. 'I'm all right, at least—' His arms went round her, drawing her close and she hid her face against his chest, not wanting him to see the helpless love that welled up in her eyes, naked and vulnerable. He rubbed his cheek against her hair and when he spoke she felt his lips, warm against her forehead.

'Oh, Nicola. I can't believe that you didn't know I loved you all those years ago at Bishop's Wood,' he said. 'That you never knew how much I wanted to take you in my arms when you looked at me with that magic glow in your eyes. I tried to tell you before but it all came out wrong.' He looked down at her. 'You can't imagine how I felt when you'd smile at me with those huge green eyes of yours, offering—without knowing—all I'd ever longed for—everything my marriage lacked. Sometimes thinking of you was the only thing that kept me sane. When you left I thought I'd never see you again and I knew that it was the best thing that could happen for both of us. After Claudia—after it happened I told myself I'd never marry again—that I expected too much of a wife—that my lifestyle was too demanding, but I know now that they were just excuses because I couldn't have you. The day I looked up and saw you at the interview I was shocked. I panicked because I thought I may have imagined it all—that you'd have made your own life by now. I couldn't stand the thought of seeing you every day and knowing I'd lost you so I tried to stop you getting the job. Later it was Maria who made me see that nothing had changed. I began to think then that maybe I could begin again—with you.'

She looked up at him with brimming eyes, almost unable to believe what she was hearing. 'I didn't understand, Simon, I thought—'

He shook his head. 'I know what you thought. Perhaps you see now that asking you to marry me wasn't the wild impulse you imagined it to be. I feel as though I've loved you for most of my life, Nicola. I can't remember a time when I didn't want you.' Swiftly he bent to kiss her, his lips betraying his hunger for her and she melted against him, responding with all the longing that was in her.

'All I wanted was to hear you say you loved me,' she whispered as their lips parted.

'I tried—on the night I asked you to marry me. But it seemed too much to hope that what you felt for me before—that magic that used to shine in your eyes would still be there. I hoped that perhaps you'd marry me for Maria's sake.' He smiled down at her wistfully. 'Life does cruel things to us as we get older, Nicola. It destroys our trust—makes us cynical.'

'The magic *is* still there,' she told him as she stood on tiptoe to kiss him. 'It always will be. I love you more now than ever, Simon—more than I ever thought possible.'

Hand in hand they walked away from the path to where the trees gathered closely, where the fallen leaves made a thick, golden carpet.

'I love this place,' she said. 'Let's stay here for a while—let's make it our special place, darling.'

In his eager arms, at one with the strength of his body she felt her spirit sing. Everything she was— that she could ever be was his for as long as she lived and as they walked back to the car later, arms round each other, she promised herself deep inside that it would always be this way.

As they came out onto the hilltop again the light had begun to fade. Below, the lights were coming on one by one, piercing the soft dusk with their brilliance. Simon pulled her close against his side as they stood looking down.

'How soon will you marry me?' he asked softly. 'I'm so afraid that something will happen to take you from me again. I feel as though I'd like to hide away with you here so that no one could ever find us.'

She smiled up at him happily. 'There's no need. Nothing can ever part us now.'

They watched as the lights came on below them. Around them darkness fell almost without their noticing and Nicola pressed closer, her head on his shoulder. It was a moment she would cherish for the rest of her life.

A very special gift for Mother's Day

You love Mills & Boon romances. Your mother will love this attractive Mother's Day gift pack. First time in paperback, four superb romances by leading authors. A very special gift for Mother's Day.

United Kingdom £4.40   On sale from 24th Feb 1984

A Grand Illusion   **Sensual Encounter**
Maura McGiveny   Carole Mortimer
Desire in the Desert   **Aquamarine**
Mary Lyons   Madeleine Ker

Look for this gift pack where you buy Mills & Boon romances.